Nigel Gray was born in Northern Ireland and brought to England as a child. After leaving school he worked for eleven years in numerous unskilled jobs. He went to the University of Lancaster as a mature student and was awarded a B.A. He is a poet, playwright and children's writer, and he has been an actor and a photographer. A collection of short stories, *Life Sentence,* was published in 1984 and will shortly be available from Futura. *Happy Families* is his first novel for adults.

Nigel Gray

HAPPY FAMILIES

Futura

A Futura Book

Copyright © Nigel Gray 1985

First published in Great Britain in 1985
by Macmillan London Ltd

This edition published in 1986 by Futura Publications,
a Division of Macdonald & Co (Publishers) Ltd
London & Sydney

ISBN 0 7088 2995 3

The author and publishers wish to thank Acuff Rose Music
Ltd. (U.K. Publisher) for permission to quote from "Bye
Bye Love" by Felice and Boudleaux Bryant. Copyright 1957
by Acuff Rose Publications Inc.

Printed in Great Britain by
The Guernsey Press Co. Ltd
Guernsey, Channel Islands

Futura Publications
a Division of
Macdonald & Co (Publishers) Ltd
Greater London House
Hampstead Road
London NW1 7QX

A BPCC plc Company

For Yasmin, who deserves a better,
and a gentler, book.

I had been sent to fetch two eggs from the cupboard for our dinner. I carried them, one in each hand, downstairs and through the living room used by the old lady who owned the house. She was sitting, as always, like a corpse in her armchair near the fire. (On the day she died I came home from school and passed her by four times without realising she was dead.)

I went into the kitchen carrying, carefully, my precious cargo. Then the egg in my right hand broke. The shell must have been paper-thin. My mother was doing the washing (a job I couldn't do because, when it was full of water, the galvanised grey bath was too heavy for me to lift onto the stove). She was prodding with the wrong end of a wooden spoon at a white sheet that was ballooning out of the blubbing water. The handle of the wooden spoon (which she called her copper stick) was bleached as white as the sheet.

The egg broke in my hand. I stared down in disbelief at the crumpled shell and at the egg's mucus oozing between my fingers – transparent streaked with orange, and in the orange a trace of blood. She saw what had happened and stopped her stabbing, staring first at my polluted hand and then at my panic-stricken face. She came at me clutching the washed-out copper stick in her white-knuckled fist. Behind her the dirty water was boiling angrily in the tub, spilling, hissing, onto the stove.

'Why did you do that?' she said, her voice shaking with the effort of self-control. 'Why can't you be more careful?' I looked up fearfully into her furious face and heard her voice rise and break. 'Can't you do one little thing right?' And then she was hitting me, beating me till the copper stick broke. She stood to catch her breath leaning with one hand against the table, staring at the bowl of the spoon hanging on a splinter like a wooden fish dangling from a toy rod. She glared at me with hatred brimming from bulging eyes and hurled the broken

7

spoon at my head. 'Now look what you've done!' she screamed, and set about slapping me with her hands until she was too weak to carry on. And through it all the second egg was protected in the snug nest of my palm.

Suddenly I realised that Sophie was crying upstairs. I sat for a moment trying to pull myself together. I didn't hear the slap Doris next door gave her son, but I heard the boy cry out and I flinched. I wearily climbed the dark stairs to pick up the crying baby from the cot.

Sophie continued to cry as I carried her down. I took off her wet nappy and her dress and held her naked on my hip as I heated water in the kettle. She cried on. She didn't stop till I'd poured the warm water into the sink and stood her gently in it. She was still for a while, fascinated by the feel of the water lapping around her chubby legs. Then I sat her carefully down and she began to splash the water with her hands. I wiped the tears from her cheeks and the snot from her nose with the teacloth and talked to her. 'I'm sorry, Sophie, love. I'd take your bath into the yard and let you play in the sun, but the stink's too bad today. We brought you into a stinking world, Sophie, and I'm sorry – we should never've done it.'

I kissed the soft fine hair of her warm head. She reached out and grasped a silvery spoon from the draining board and hit the water with it. She laughed. I jumped back and cried out pretending she'd splashed me. And she laughed louder. I leaned forward and thrust my face over the sink. She hit out with the spoon, screwing up her eyes against the leaping water. I bounded back and we laughed. And again. And again. And we laughed and laughed so much she couldn't splash the water for laughing. I hadn't heard that full, uninhibited laugh for days, and her laughing made me cry.

She played in the water for nearly an hour, and then, when she got bored, I lifted her out and dried her. I carried her into the living room and spread the towel on the lino. I laid her on her stomach on the towel and sat on the floor beside her. I shook her rattle so that she held up her head to look at it and then I placed it six inches out of her reach. She struggled and wriggled and rested and writhed and folded herself up and stretched out again until at last she managed to clasp it in her hand and put it to her mouth.

'Sophie baby, you got it. There's a clever girl. If only your mummy could see you. She'd be so proud of you.' I sat her up and held my hand out for the rattle and said, 'Ta,' and she gave it to me. I gave it back. And she gave it to me again. And so on. 'You're a clever girl,' I said. 'Do you know that?' I clapped my hands loudly and she replied by clapping hers in silent applause. I laid her down and put the rattle about a foot in front of her. She struggled to get to it like a turtle trying to get back to the sea. When she finally reached it I picked her up, delighted, and cuddled her and kissed her face. She took hold of my bottom lip in her hand scratching me with her sharp finger-nails. 'Daddy loves you,' I said. 'You're a beautiful girl, and Daddy loves you more than anything in the whole wide world.'

I put off feeding her for as long as possible. I wanted her small ration of happiness to last. I stood at the front room window in the dusk holding her and pointing out fascinating characters and scenes in the drama of our street. People were coming home from work, others stood gossiping in groups or sat on their front steps. Children were running and shouting, playing skipping and two-balls, hopscotch and football. Dogs and pigeons, cats and cars played supporting roles, and in the backcloth of the terrace opposite, windows here and there were magically lighting up. Then we walked around the house looking at the things there were to see. Just ordinary things – but everything is of interest to a baby. I told her what each object was called. 'Hairbrush. This is a hairbrush. Shall I brush your hair? Do you want to brush Daddy's hair? This is matches, a box of matches. Shake it. Makes a nice rattle, see.' We played boo with ourselves in the mirror and looked behind the mirror to see if we were on the other side. I threw her up to the ceiling and caught her. I sang songs to her and bounced her on my knees. But finally she cried because she was tired and hungry and would be distracted no more.

I carried her into the kitchen on my hip, singing softly to her. I poured milk into a saucepan and set it on the stove. I turned on the gas, struck a match and put it under the saucepan and the gas whooped alight. I held up the burning match for Sophie to see the dancing flame. She stopped crying to look at it. Then the flame died.

I dropped the match onto the floor and moved the saucepan to centre it above the gas burner. I took the sedative that the doctor had prescribed for Sheila out of the kitchen cabinet. I unscrewed the top of the medicine bottle keeping it, with difficulty, out of Sophie's grasping reach, and poured the grey syrup into the baby's bottle till it was one third full. I left the medicine bottle on the draining board without bothering to replace the cap. I dipped a finger into the milk heating in the saucepan. The milk was at body temperature. I could feel nothing. Nothing. I turned the gas off and poured warm milk from the saucepan into Sophie's bottle. I screwed on the top with its yellow teat and wiped the bottle with a teacloth. I turned the bottle upside down over the sink and shook it vigorously so that the syrup would mix with the milk, and a thin jet of white spurted out like a monkey's spunk. Sophie was crying loudly. I put the bottle to her mouth and she sucked eagerly at it as though she knew it would take away her pain, and she was quiet. She took her mouth away and cried again a couple more cries and went back to sucking at the teat.

Later, sitting with the baby still in my lap, I must have dozed because I suddenly found myself confused. I thought I was in bed with Sheila. I must have been dreaming, but I couldn't remember what the dream was about.

Sheila woke me from a dream. I was in a bare cell and a man was trying to force me to put on a uniform. But I refused. Then a boot, twice as big as a normal man's foot, blasted furiously into my chest and I fell on my back on the cold flagstone floor. I was naked. The man went out and slammed the cell door.

Sheila was sitting up in bed so the covers were pulled away from my chest and shoulders. She was saying something to me. I kept trying to wake up but sleep wouldn't let me go. It was like trying to climb out of a pit while someone was continually grabbing my ankles and dragging me back down. Eventually she lay down again. She was angry. I gave up the struggle and let sleep suck me into its depths.

Sheila woke me again. It was still dark. 'It's started,' she was saying. 'It's started. You've got to do something.' I rolled out of bed and began getting into my clothes. I felt dizzy and sat on the edge of the mattress for a moment with my head between my knees. 'Hurry, Paul, hurry!' she said. 'Something's happening. Get the ambulance.' I couldn't find my jeans. I groped for the light switch. Before I'd got my shoes tied the electricity went. I knew there was a shilling on the mantelpiece in the front room so I felt my way downstairs. I fumbled and stumbled in a panic of darkness. Sheila started shouting down the stairs. 'Paul! For God's sake! Hurry up!'

'I'm putting the fucking lights on.'

'Never mind the lights. Get the ambulance!'

'But then you'll be left in the dark.'

'It doesn't matter.'

She had reason to be worried about the birth.

It was a long way to the phone box. It was drizzling, and cold. I ran over the wet cobbles of the back alley trying to avoid the dog shit, relieved to be out of the house.

Two years earlier, when I was eighteen, I'd run out from

another house in another town to phone for an ambulance in the night. Laura's baby, my first child, Josephine, was six weeks overdue (unless of course Laura, the girl I lived with then, had tricked me into taking her back by telling me she was already pregnant when she wasn't). In any case, after a year and a half of Laura's histrionics and six weeks of disappointed daily anticipation I didn't believe it was actually happening. Laura was sixteen years old and scared. I allowed her to be bundled off alone into the unknown and went back to bed and sleep. The following morning I phoned the hospital and heard that my baby had already been born. I felt then like a dog that's shat on the sitting room carpet.

I went with Sheila in the ambulance and carried her case up the ether-smelling hospital stairway.

'Stay with me, Paul,' she said.

'Yeah. 'Course I will.'

We were in a small bright room. There were two beds, two screens folded against the wall, a sink, a cupboard, a trolley laden with hospital paraphernalia. A pink nurse bustled in, small and round and officious. 'I'm sorry, you'll have to leave now.'

'I'm going to stay ...'

'You can't stay. Out you go.'

'I'm staying.'

'The doctor won't have anybody here who isn't needed. You'll just get in the way.'

'I *am* needed. She wants me to stay with her.'

'Out of the question.' She was propelling me in fits and starts towards the door. I could see Sheila's panic-stricken face behind her, but short of using force and risking an undignified wrestling bout with the little nurse there was nothing I could do.

'I want him with me,' Sheila said.

''Fraid it's not allowed.'

'Whose baby is it, anyhow?' I blurted.

'Sorry. Hospital regulations.'

'I'm not interested in regulations. I'm interested in her welfare.'

'Just wait outside, please, while we get her ready.'

I was in the corridor and the door closed. I heard Sheila cry

13

out my name. I called back, 'It's all right, love, I'm here.' The nurse came out of the room with one of the screens which she unfolded across the corridor. She began pushing it gently but firmly against me, edging me backwards. I hadn't the confidence in the face of her authority to resist, but I wouldn't move of my own accord. I felt pathetic.

'Will you please go now,' the nurse said from behind the screen.

'No. I won't.'

'Sorry, but you have to go. Telephone at midday.'

When she had forced me to the head of the stairs she went back to the room. I peered round the edge of the screen. From somewhere came a woman's scream. There was some coming and going and then they wheeled Sheila out of the room into the ward at the far end of the corridor. Some time later Sheila started shouting for me. I was in two minds as to whether to go to look for her or not. I wasn't sure that she was still in the ward. I was afraid of blundering into the wrong room. I imagined how awful it would be for some woman if a strange man came barging in while she was giving birth. I contented myself with shouting back that I was still there; that I was close by. A pretty West Indian nurse came and told me crossly to be quiet. She said I was disturbing the patients. I said, 'I will be quiet if you'll let me sit with her. She needs me. She needs someone with her. Don't you know what she's been through already?'

'We'll take care of her,' she said in her bedside manner.

'But you're not taking care of her. You're making her tense and frightened. I don't know if you know her case history. She hasn't had just an ordinary pregnancy, you know. She needs to be relaxed. If I sit with her I can help her.'

'She'll be all right.' She said it reassuringly, as if she was talking to an over-excited village idiot.

'She's not bloody all right. You're all the same, you people. She's not a bloody machine or something.'

'Will you please be quiet!' The cross schoolteacher now to the obstreperous infant. She turned and walked back to the ward.

I remained on duty behind the screen for a further two hours. Just after eight the nice-looking black nurse came back. She started folding the screen away, unveiling me. I felt startled and

14

exposed. She smiled. 'You're very obstinate, aren't you?' she said. 'Do you want to see her now?'

I followed her along to the delivery room. I didn't know they'd taken Sheila back there. The little bossy nurse passed me in the doorway and smiled at me. Sheila was lying in the bed looking pale, tired, and happy.

'Are you all right?' I asked.

I took hold of both her hands as she looked up at me, smiling. Tears came into her eyes and she nodded. 'It was easy. I wish you'd been here.'

'Oh, yes. I wish . . . and the baby?'

'There's nothing wrong with her.' Her voice, full of disbelief, overflowed into tears which formed pools either side of her nose and ran slowly down her face. 'She's perfect. I held her.'

Exhaustion disabled me. It was as if dread had been holding me erect all those months and it had suddenly been dragged out, like stuffing from a toy bear. I slumped onto a chair by the bed. We gazed into each other's eyes, crying and smiling at the same time, creating our own rainbow.

I began shaking my head stupidly like a circus elephant. 'You're so clever,' I said. 'You know that?'

'Am I? Oh, tell me.'

'You're so clever. You're . . . you made her perfect. Despite everything.'

'I didn't have gas, or stitches, or anything.'

The nurse said, 'You'd better go now. She needs to sleep.'

'I'm going to breastfeed her,' Sheila said.

'Of course you are,' I said. 'I'll see you later. Sleep well, clever girl.' I kissed her and followed the nurse into the corridor wiping my face with my hands.

The nurse put the tiny, ugly, beautiful baby into my hands. When I'd first held Josephine I was frightened of her fragility. But when I first held Sophie I felt only gratitude for what I mistook for good fortune. She was alive, whole, healthy. Now I realise that fortune was playing a cruel trick. Had she been smiling on me, the baby would have been born dead.

I wonder, now, how it was that I brought two perfect daughters into the world. Certainly it was never my intention. You can only plan for the future. I have always been looking backwards and running away from what was behind me.

When I was a little boy, undernourished and weakly, I was punished daily by women who were bigger than me. In my teens I shot up suddenly like a tropical plant in the hot sun that follows heavy rain. I went out with women of my own age, and I was bigger than them. Conscious of the power in my prick, I punished them. As a consequence I found myself trapped twice before I was twenty. Wisdom came like a ball and chain.

The second conception I was responsible for was no more immaculate than the first. In fact despite my feelings being clean and clear, it was even more muddled and muddy. I'd rented a room from a clerk who worked in the warehouse where I loaded my lorry. Soon after, I got laid off and had to sign on. As a result I spent a lot of time around his wife. I became fast friends with her, and fancied her too, although I felt she was clearly above my class. Sheila was twenty-three, four years older than me, and she was the loveliest woman I'd ever met. There was a richness about her, a Mother Earth quality. If the girls I'd known before were willow and mountain ash, she was a copper beech in full maturity. But she seemed vulnerable too, in the way, I suppose, that wood is defenceless against the axe.

In the mornings, I'd lie in my room and hear them talking downstairs. Then I'd hear the back door bang, Tom's footsteps, and the car door slam. Starter whirr, starter whirr, starter, rev, rev, rev, and the whine of the car's reverse onto the road before driving off and fading into the distance. Alone with Sheila in the house, I'd hear her step-stepping up the stairs and her soft knock-knock on my door. Every morning, before she dressed, she brought me a mug of tea, and then, while the tea cooled, I'd masturbate with the memory of her still warm, until I felt cold fingers of guilt slide across my stomach to stain my bed.

As I came downstairs I saw Sheila, like a Siren, lying with her long auburn hair flowing across the sea of green carpet. I was drawn to her and sat beside her on the floor. 'You look unhappy,' I said.

'Do I?'

'What's the matter?'

'I tried to talk to Tom last night.'

'Tried?'

'He won't . . . he avoids things all the time. I begged him to stay home with me today. But he wouldn't. Said he had to go to work.'

There was silence, except for the hissing of the gas fire. With a sensual serpent-like movement she twisted towards me, then lay still like a cat curled softly in sleep. I began to stroke her hair where it lay across the carpet. 'I like people to touch my hair,' she said. She turned her face to look up at me. 'It's so nice having you here. You've no idea how lonely it is being in a house all day on your own. All your unhappiness is locked inside. Eating you away. And you never say it. Never speak it out. You put it away. Try to forget it. Turn it in on yourself.' She spoke slowly, haltingly, and her forehead was furrowed with the effort of searching for appropriate words. She lowered her eyes from my face. 'I feel so happy with you here. You make me feel . . . attractive. The way you look at me. I feel . . . all . . . tingly. Like electricity in my body.'

'You surely don't need *me* to make you feel attractive. You're the most beautiful woman I've ever known.'

'I feel so ugly most of the time.'

'How can you feel ugly?'

'Tom . . . doesn't seem to like me. He doesn't like making love to me.' She started to cry. 'He hardly ever . . . I get tired and say I want to go to bed. And he says, "You go on up. I'll be up in a

18

minute. I just want to have a look at the paper." Then he sits down here and reads for a couple of hours. Till maybe two in the morning. And even when he *does*, he doesn't like touching me. I know he doesn't. As soon as we've made love he moves away. Right over the other side of the bed so that our bodies aren't touching. It makes me feel my body must be repulsive.'

I raised her up and hugged her, resting my cheek on the thick soft hair of her head, rocking her backwards and forwards. After a while she stopped crying and we sat with our arms around each other. When I spoke my voice was hoarse. 'Why did you marry him?'

'I don't know. I just wanted to get married. I was still at school. Tom was the first person I actually went all the way with. He was eight years older than me. He didn't want to get married, really. I forced him, I suppose.'

'Did you love him?'

'He was such a steady, secure sort of person. He made me feel safe. I thought I could work at loving him. That if I worked hard we would grow to love each other. But we haven't. I've tried. He's nice to me. But it hasn't really worked.'

'Sounds like you wanted a father more than a husband.'

She looked up at me. Her eyes were wet and tears had left snail's trails down her cheeks. 'Do you think so? I never thought of that before.' I wiped the wetness from her cheeks with my finger and she nuzzled her head against me. 'My father left when I was five. I used to visit him sometimes, but we never seemed to be able to talk to each other. He was so cold. So unemotional. I could never seem to get him to notice me. I wanted to ... to break through to him, but I never could.'

'Perhaps you need a lover.'

'I've tried that.'

'Wasn't it any good?'

'It just made everything worse. One of Tom's friends ... oh, he was horrible. I don't want to talk about it. Then there was a mature student at college. He'd been out in Africa somewhere. And one of the lecturers. He was the worst. That went on for ages.'

'What do you mean, worst?'

'Oh. He was so nasty. Sometimes he'd want me. Sometimes he wouldn't. And he ... you know ... didn't bother. Once,

I asked him if he'd zip me up, and he said, "My job's undoing it, not doing it up." It just made it worse. They made me feel more ugly than ever. None of them really wanted *me*. I was just a safe fuck because I was a married woman.'

'What did Tom think about it?'

'I don't know. He's funny. He must know. I never told him outright, but I didn't make any secret of it. He knew I was going out with them, and they came here, and we messed around and everything. He almost seemed to encourage it, as though it took some of the responsibility off his hands. Then other times he says things as though he doesn't suspect anything at all.'

Sheila and I became as thick as thieves. When we were together Tom was like an outsider, and later an intruder, into *our* home. Eventually, one evening during a late meal, he asked me to leave. Sheila stared at him as though he had just condemned the two of us to death. 'Why?' she demanded.

'I ... well ... we've got people coming for Christmas and ...'

'Where's Paul supposed to go?'

'Look, Sheila ... I don't know.'

'Why do you want him to go?'

'I just ...'

'Why? I don't want him to leave.'

There was a short silence. Then Sheila started clearing the table, crashing and clanging dishes and cutlery. Tom and I sat chasing potatoes around our plates with our knives and forks. After dinner Sheila went up to bed. I sat up with Tom but he didn't talk. After a while he said he was going out. He drove off fast. I sat for a bit, then turned the fire off and crept quietly upstairs. Sheila was alone in her bedroom. I stopped by the door. I could hear her crying. I went to my room and went to bed.

Sheila woke me in the morning as usual with a mug of tea. She was wearing a white nightdress. I could see her nipples nudging the thin material. She sat on the edge of my bed and I was shocked by how old and ill she looked. Her eyes were red with crying. 'Did we keep you awake?' she asked. I shook my head. 'I told him about ... everything,' she said. 'I wanted to be really honest with him. Since you've come ... I don't know. I just wanted to be honest. We've been living a lie so long. So many lies. I tried to tell him, like I told you.'

'What did he say?'

'He kept trying to stop me. He didn't want to hear. Then he got angry. I've never seen him so angry. He threatened to hit

21

me if I didn't shut up. He's never done that before. I said he must have known. He said he never thought anything like that was going on.'

'What happened?'

'He told me to clear off. I cried. Then he got these terrible stomach cramps and couldn't sleep. I asked him to stay home with me today. But he wouldn't.'

'Why did you want him to stay home?'

She didn't reply, but looked at me as if the answer was obvious. I wanted her to say it but she didn't. I felt myself begin to tremble with anticipation. I thought she was going to get into **my bed, but she made no move.**

'If he told you to clear out, why don't you?' I said. She closed her eyes and her head drooped as if it was too heavy for her to bear its weight. 'Will you come with *me*?' My voice was shaky and gruff.

'No.'

'Why?'

'I'm married.'

'What does that mean?'

'I don't know.' She started gnawing at the skin on the side of her thumbnail. 'I think I told him those things because I want him to be jealous. I want him to notice me.'

'Is that why you want me here? To make Tom jealous?'

She looked at me hard. She was chewing. A little piece of her own skin I suppose. She opened her mouth, but didn't say anything. She shook her head, turning away. 'I don't know,' she said.

She got up and went out of the room. I could hear her moving about in her bedroom. A few moments earlier, I'd thought the prize was mine for the taking, but it seemed to have been snatched away leaving me undefended and empty handed. Loneliness closed in on me like an iron maiden. To ease the pain I got up and pulled the curtains back. There was condensation on the glass and an insipid fog outside. I stood gazing at nothing. Then I saw the kid in the house opposite: jumping up and down. He was about eighteen months. His cot stood by the window. He was always in that damn cot, any time of the day you looked. The cot had bars on the side. The house was clean. The garden correct. The car immaculate. The young

22

couple consummate. But the kid was always stuck away upstairs in that little prison.

I heard Sheila go into the bathroom. Then the flush went. She came out and walked slowly downstairs. I realised I was cold. I got dressed and went down to the kitchen. Sheila was washing up. I stood inside the door watching her. Suddenly she stopped what she was doing, turned towards me and burst into a torrent of tears. I held my arms out to her. She came and clutched onto me. I held her, rocking slightly, kissing her hair, her face pressed into my chest. I nudged her face up, kissed her forehead, her salt-wet eyes and cheeks, her mouth. We were kissing, clinging onto each other as if we stood in the centre of a cyclone. I was shaking. The kettle was boiling, steam filling the kitchen. She tore herself away. Turned off the gas. Led me up to the bedroom by the hand. She undressed and got into bed as naturally as if we'd been married for a year. Her body was as soft and warm as a sleeping cat. The smell of her skin seemed to fill a hollow inside my head. We intertwined, involved and absorbed in each other. The lips between her thighs were as soft, warm, and wet as the lips of her mouth. I sucked her breasts like a starving baby desperate for life. I started to stroke her cunt with my cock, but each down-stroke took me between her lips and, though I didn't want to come into her yet, the warmth and electricity drew me in deeper and deeper than I meant to and I was fucking her, holding back the fullness that was trying to foam into her so that the feeling would go on and on, but couldn't make it last any longer at last, and it discharged into the warm depths of her softness, and my strength drained away, and I sank onto her, my mouth onto hers, and lay still inside her, open mouth to mouth, heartbeat and breathing gradually easing.

Every day I went to the house and Sheila and I made love. I always left before Tom came home, to save him embarrassment. I spent the nights in a sleeping-bag in the back of my van parked on the marshes about a mile away. When Tom was home and I couldn't go to the house, Sheila usually managed to come to me. She brought food and we fucked in the back of the van. Then she decided not to see me any more. She was determined to make it work with Tom. I felt bitter and betrayed and in need of a dark place I could withdraw into to lick my weeping wounds.

I found a caravan on an almost abandoned site, and from there I sent Sheila a single love letter. It was three weeks before she replied, and the reply said simply, 'Come at once.' We made love on the green carpet. Afterwards, Sheila said, 'Take me back with you.'

'Now?'

'Tonight. I'll talk to Tom first.'

That evening I went back to the house to collect her, and to confront Tom. I rang the front door bell. Sheila led me into the living room and went upstairs to pack her things.

'What do you want?' Tom said.

'The thing is, Tom,' I said, 'Sheila and I want to be together.' Sitting hunched in his chair, he seemed smaller than when I first knew him at work. More like my girlfriend's father than my lover's husband. His face was a wooden mask staring fixedly into a bleak future. He tapped his fingers on the arm of his chair. 'I wish you would believe I'm not doing this to hurt you,' I said.

'I don't want to hear.'

'None of us can help what we feel.'

'I don't want to listen.'

'Well . . . what about . . . why don't we live together – all of us?'

24

'What?'

'All three of us.'

'You're mad.'

'That way you wouldn't lose anything. You wouldn't lose Sheila.'

'I don't want to discuss it.' Tom sat trapped in his chair, lips compressed, gazing at nothing, fingers drumming, like a condemned man awaiting electrocution.

'Tom. We always got along great. I don't want to push you out in the cold.'

'I'm not interested. I want you to go. I don't want you in my house.'

'Look, Tom, I'm making an offer for *you*. For your sake. The fact is, Sheila's going to live with me.'

'She's my wife. She's staying here.'

Sheila came down the stairs with a suitcase in her hand. 'I'm not, Tom,' she said. 'I'm going.'

'I want you out,' Tom said without looking at me. 'I don't want to see you here again.'

'Sheila's coming with me, Tom.'

'Sheila's married to me. She's staying. We were perfectly all right till you came along.'

'For God's sake, Tom,' Sheila said, 'why don't you open your eyes? Why won't you face the truth? We weren't. *You* weren't happy. *I* wasn't happy. *Nothing* was all right.'

Tom stared ahead, tapping his fingers frantically on the arms of his chair. 'Everything was perfectly all right till you came along. You caused all this. Just get out. And stay away from my wife.'

Sheila moved deliberately into the line of Tom's vision but he didn't seem to see her. 'Tom, I'm going. I'm going with Paul.' She looked scared. Tom stared and tapped. 'Bye, Tom,' she said.

At the caravan, Sheila waited by the door while I groped for the matches and lit the gas lights. She looked ill. I sat her down, still with her coat on. It was musty, damp and cold in there. I put the kettle on, pulled the bed down out of the wall, and made the tea. 'Well, here we are,' I said. She held onto her mug with both hands, making no reply, sitting huddled into her coat, as still as death. I wouldn't have known she was breathing except I could see wisps of her breath like cigarette smoke in the cold air. I sipped my tea in silence and then undressed her and helped her into the chilled sheets. She did whatever I told her like an automaton. I hugged her in bed trying to warm her. 'This should be a wonderful moment,' I said. 'But there's no joy in it at all.'

'I'm worried about Tom.'

'I know.'

'I don't know what to do.'

She cried quietly. I cuddled her for a long time. Then fucked her as gently as I could.

The next day was depressing. Sheila was eaten up with guilt. In the evening she wanted to go to see Tom. I drove her over and sat in the van outside. She was gone a long time. Then she came running out, shouting, 'Quick! Paul! Quick!'

'What's the matter?'

'Come quick!' I ran into the house and followed her through to the kitchen. Tom sat on a chair looking surprised and pale. He gripped his left wrist in his right hand and was holding it away from his body as if it offended him. Blood was running down his fingers and dropping onto the floor.

'Jesus wept! I'll get an ambulance.' I started to go, then turned back. Sheila was tying a cloth round Tom's wrist. 'Never mind waiting for an ambulance,' I said. 'Let's go in the van.'

The Outpatients Department was practically deserted. The woman who took Tom's particulars didn't seem perturbed despite the blood that was dripping from him like rain off an umbrella in a thunderstorm. I suppose she was used to worse. A doctor soon came and took Tom into a room and closed the door. Sheila and I sat together waiting. She looked like a corpse – as though his blood had drained out of *her*. I put my arm round her to comfort her but she remained rigid, so I took my arm away and held her hand instead. 'What happened, for Christ's sake?'

'He punched his fist through the window.'

'What'd he do that for?'

'He said if I left him he'd do himself in. I told him not to be so melodramatic. Then he punched his fist through the glass in the back door.'

Tom had not only opened an artery, but also severed a ligament and a nerve.

They kept him in for three weeks. Sheila and I stayed at her house. There was no joy. We cuddled or fucked for comfort rather than pleasure. Sheila looked increasingly sick as the days passed. Every evening I drove her to the hospital and waited outside while she sat with Tom. He never wanted to know where I was or what I was doing. When I asked what she would do when Tom came home she said she didn't know.

One night after visiting, and driving home without speaking, she sat on the floor of the living room in front of the gas fire, staring. I made some cocoa and squatted beside her. She said, 'Tom's coming out tomorrow.'

'Oh.'

'What am I going to do?'

I shrugged. 'You must do what you want.'

'How can I? Everyone's making demands on me. I can't take any more. I can't. You want me to go with you. Tom wants me to stay.'

'That's why you have to do what *you* want.'

'How do I know what I want?'

'Do you think you'll be happy if you stay?'

'Of course not. It would be like coming back to prison.'

'Well, don't go back to prison.'

'And supposing he does something else?'

'That's his decision. That's nothing to do with you. You must make your decisions, he must make his.'

'But how could I be happy with you if Tom ... ?'

'You've got to find your happiness where you can.'

'But there's nowhere. I'm trapped. Oh, Paul, please tell me what to do. If you tell me to go with you, I will.'

'You've got to make your own decisions.' She was biting

frantically at her fingers. The corners of her nails were red-raw and swollen. 'Don't do that.' I tried to tear her hand away from her teeth but she twisted away angrily and went on gnawing. 'Will it make it easier for you if *I* go away?' I asked.

'Is that what you want?'

'No.'

'You're fed up with me.'

'No.'

'You want to go.'

'No.'

'You want to leave me.'

She was holding onto me now. I grabbed her shoulders and shook her. 'No. I keep telling you, fucking no! I want to live with you. I'm asking would it be easier for *you*?'

She became deflated again, like a balloon a week after Christmas. 'Paul?'

'What?'

'When I stopped seeing you, I wanted to make it work with Tom. I thought if I stopped taking my pills it would make sure I wouldn't weaken and sleep with you again. I wrote because I needed to talk to you, but when you came and started to kiss me, I couldn't say no. My body was screaming yes. Oh, Paul. I think I'm pregnant.'

I stared at her in a state of shock, hardly able to recognise in her the woman I'd loved and lusted after. My once beautiful and bountiful mistress had degenerated into a white-faced hag with red-rimmed eyes and bleeding finger-ends. 'I think I'm pregnant,' she repeated. 'What am I going to do, what am I going to do, what am I going to do . . . ?' Her voice mounted a stairway to screaming pitch. I tried to take hold of her to comfort her but she fought me off, screeching the words over and over until they disintegrated through unintelligibility into loud ugly cries. It was like listening to living pain straining to burst out of a steel-clamped container. I sat on the floor watching helplessly as she lay face down on the carpet making a noise like a crow having its wings torn off.

Later, in bed, I asked her if she was sure.

'Yes,' she said. 'My period hasn't come.'

'Maybe it's just late.'

'I know my own body, Paul.'

I hugged her for a while and then started to fondle her. She tried to force my hand away but I wouldn't let her.

'Paul, you're hurting.'

'Stop pushing me off then.'

'I don't feel like it tonight.'

'Well, I do.'

'Please don't. I don't want to.'

I felt hurt and rejected. Bitter anger was a bad taste in my mouth. I fucked her. She lay like death warmed up, with her face turned away.

When I woke she was already up. I dressed and went downstairs. She was sitting at the kitchen table sipping coffee. She didn't speak, or even look up.

'Well, what's happening?' I sat opposite her, waiting for an answer.

'Tom's coming home today.'

'What are you going to do?'

'I'm staying.'

'What about me?'

She made no reply.

'And the baby?'

'What baby?'

'I thought you were pregnant.'

'There's not going to any baby.'

'What do you mean?'

'I'll have an abortion.'

She looked ugly. She was biting the inside of her cheek, twisting her mouth to the side. She had a red headless boil swelling on her chin. She looked old. She could have been my mother. I got up and went round the table to her. She didn't move. I bent down and kissed her on the head pressing my face into her thick hair. 'If you change your mind,' I said, 'I'll be at the caravan.' And when she made no response, I added, 'I love you.'

But she had already petrified. Though familiar, she had become a stranger.

When I first went to live with my mother, she lodged in a back bedroom of a terraced house near the cattle market. We shared the room, the woman and myself, though we were strangers. I was a strange child. Hardly childlike at all. Quiet and sullen. I unnerved her by following her movements with eyes narrowed in the closed wall of my face like loop-holes in a battlement.

I always did as I was told, but she read defiance in my eyes. I could see her anger becoming inflamed each time she caught sight of that glow among the ashes. She wanted to stamp on it like you would stamp out a small fire in a forest before it flared out of control. She hated yet respected me for it because it was a reflection of the defiant smouldering in her own eyes. She despised and feared me at the same time, the way Stalin must have despised and feared people in *his* power.

I was all that was left of her unwanted brood. The remnant of her longed-for family. The last vestige of the misery of her marriage, of the fairy story where no one lived happily ever after. I was frosted and defended, impenetrable, reminding her of the boy she still loved and hated so much. The boy with the ice-hard penetrating eyes, who found her, felt her, fucked her, forgot her, left her more arid, more alone, more afraid than before. I was the last echo of her man and she wanted to silence him for ever. (She did not know that he was already dead.) I was made in the image of my father, and she wanted to tear me in half like an old wedding photograph.

He'd wanted to leave her with nothing. ('You're not fit to look after children,' he'd said.) But she'd got one over on him. I was hers, her souvenir, her possession. An object she would do with as she wanted. On the other hand I was a further limitation on her freedom. An extra millstone for her to carry when she already had too heavy a burden to bear. She demanded compensation for that, yet she was afraid of the hate in my eyes. She was a soldier who would violate any sanctuary to slaughter that refugee. She would have sold her soul to be able to pursue me into that secret place I fled to deep inside where nothing human could ever reach.

More than anything in the world I wanted something to love. Something to hold. Something warm. As a pass to present at the barrier I kept erected around myself she brought home a black kitten. Blackie bit and scratched, but it was beautiful because it was me she held on to. She was soft and summery and smelled of life. I buried my face in her fur. She needled my skin with tiny claws and it was marvellous because she was clinging to *me*.

For five days I knew love. Then I came home from school and couldn't find her. I searched and searched, again and again. I called and called. My mother came in later from work. 'I can't find Blackie anywhere.' I cried.

Her complexion was always unnaturally pale, so that her lipstick looked like a bloody gash across her pinched face. Her voice was a clenched fist. 'The landlady said we couldn't keep it.'

'But where's Blackie?'

'I took it to the PDSA,' she said, 'and had it put to sleep.'

(Put to sleep. So it was as easy as that.)

I stopped crying and stared at her. 'What do you mean?'

She lowered her eyes for a moment, and then, suddenly, her face flushed, and she looked straight at me and spat out the words: 'I had it destroyed.'

Destroyed.

I stuffed the cracks around the door and windows of the caravan with clothes. I turned the gas on and went to bed. I slept and dreamed and finally woke. I didn't know what day it was. The gas cylinder was empty. I felt sick and dizzy. I staggered into a three-month fog of depression. Somewhere in the haze I met a college student and carted her back to the caravan. She struggled fiercely but quietly and I managed to strip her and fuck her. There was no pleasure. But time heals and the mist started to clear. I even began to buy the local paper to look for a job. Then one morning the mail brought a note from Sheila asking me to go to see her.

As I drove over I was surprised to realise it was midsummer. The hedgerows were in full foliage narrowing the road to a single track. The fields were brimming with barley and the spring's babies were already growing fat.

When she opened the door she clung onto me as if I was a lifebelt and she was in danger of drowning in the flood of her own tears. She looked ill and there were dark bags under her swollen eyes. 'I'm so glad you've come. So glad you've come. I've been wanting you so much. So much.'

We went in and sat on the floor holding onto one another. Her tears kept flowing like ice melting in spring. 'Will you take me to the hospital this afternoon?'

'Of course. What for?'

'To see the specialist.'

'What specialist?'

'About the abortion.'

'Haven't you had it yet?'

'No.'

'Isn't it too late now?'

'I don't know.'

'How far gone are you?'

33

'Nearly four months.'

'Why didn't you have it before?'

'I lost all this blood in the street – gallons of it. The doctor said I'd miscarried. He didn't even examine me. But afterwards – after a couple of weeks – I was sure I was still pregnant so I went for a test at the clinic and it was positive. I knew. I knew I was.'

'Jesus wept! Why didn't he fucking examine you?'

'I don't know. He didn't.'

'I thought you couldn't get an abortion after three months.'

'You can't usually but I've had rubella.'

'You've had *what*?'

'Rubella. German measles. Oh, Paul, what can I do?'

'When did you have that?'

'Just before the miscarriage. I mean, the ... you know, the bleeding. After you left I went for a pregnancy test and it was negative. Then I caught german measles off the little girl next door. I was ill for about a week. I was sure I was pregnant so I went for another test and it was positive. I got the doctor to book me in for an abortion and then I had the bleeding and he cancelled the arrangements. Then I had another test and it was positive again. Paul, I've *got* to get rid of it.'

'Jesus fucking Christ, that doctor ought to be shot. My poor love. Why didn't you contact me?'

'Tom didn't want me to. And my mother's been staying and she said I mustn't. And, oh, I don't know. I didn't know what to do. I wanted you so much.'

'What time's the appointment?'

'Three.'

'OK.'

'People keep telling me about rubella and what it does. It deforms the baby. Oh, it's terrible. I've got something growing inside me that's all deformed. It's so horrid.'

''Course you haven't. Don't be silly.'

'They keep telling me. And I keep having these dreams about monsters with two heads and no arms. I keep dreaming I'm giving birth to monsters.'

'There's going to be no monsters. everything's going to be all right. I'll take care of you. Everything's going to be all right.'

'Oh, yes, yes, tell me. Tell me it'll be all right.'

'Sure it will. I'll stay with you. I'll look after you. Everything's going to be all right. I promise.'

'Thank you. Oh, thank you.'

'How's things here? OK?'

'No. It's awful.'

I felt pleased and guilty for being pleased. 'How do you mean, awful?'

'Tom's so nice. And I can't bear him. He makes me feel sick. I can't bear him near me. I can't bear him to touch me. I'm nasty to him but he won't be nasty back and that makes me hate him. Despise him. But he's so kind to me and I feel so guilty about loathing him the way I do.'

'You can't go on like that. Something'll have to happen. It'll be all right. We'll sort it out. Don't worry.'

We held each other for a long time. Then we started kissing. We made love there on the carpet. It was like coming home. It was like peace after all the warring that had gone on within me. But it's difficult to pick up the threads of life when you come home from a war. You find there are other wars too. Nothing is easy.

That afternoon I went with Sheila to the hospital. We were there well before three. The waiting room felt cold although the day was warm. There were no windows. Upright chairs stood around four walls and there was no air between. A few other folk waited and went when their names were called. Sheila and I seemed to have nothing to say. The hard chairs became more uncomfortable as the time passed so that the waiting room turned into a punishment cell. I picked up a women's magazine and flicked through it. There was a photo of a woman in a white summer dress sitting on a flight of whitewashed stone steps. She had blonde hair and dark blue eyes and a wide mouth with perfect teeth. Her head was cocked to one side and she smiled a warm and inviting smile. She sat with her legs apart so that her dress hung down between her thighs. Her arms and legs were bare and brown and covered with a down of hair, gold in the sunshine. I tried to soak up the picture without Sheila noticing. I was scared of her jealousy.

I wanted to go to that woman. Not to master her, or to hurt her, but to be received by her – the way, I suppose, some people want to go to a priest. She seemed to offer gentleness, and a warm, secure love. There was a mothering quality about her. I was surprised to realise suddenly that she reminded me of Sheila. Of Sheila when I first knew her.

At ten past four Sheila was called in and I went to sit in the van on the car park. When she came out just before five she was distraught.

'What's the matter? Sheila, what's the matter, love?' For a long time she couldn't speak for crying. 'It's all right. It's all right. There, there, there, there, it's all right.'

'Bastard bastard bastard bastard ...'

'What, love, what?'

'The bastard. The bastard.'

36

'What happened?'

'The pig. He was a pig. I had to strip. Then they left me for half an hour. Then he came in and pulled me about as rough as ... as if I was a cow or something. Then he ... then he ... just walked out.'

'Didn't he say anything?'

'No. The pig. I got up and ran after him and said, "Can I have an abortion or can't I?" and he wouldn't even answer. He said to the nurse, "Will you kindly tell Mrs Hill that I'll inform her GP in due course and he'll no doubt let her know my decision." And he just carried on walking.'

I felt like rushing in to find him. I wanted to feel the bone of his nose crunch under my fist. I wanted to fling his desk over, scatter his files and smash the furniture in his room. But though my emotions were storm-driven in this violent frenzy, I displayed a surface tranquillity which washed over Sheila, caressing her, soothing her, calming her.

I fell back into the pattern of going to Sheila's every day while Tom was out at work. She needed total attention and constant comforting. I had been drawn to her because I was damaged and needed her strength. Now I had to be strong to protect her fragility.

It was two weeks before the doctor informed her she could have the abortion and a further ten days before she went into hospital. I took her one Wednesday morning. Then I went to a greengrocer and got some of every sort of fruit I could find in the shop. Although it wasn't visiting time they let me take it in to her and I managed to stay twenty minutes before they turfed me out.

She'd forgotten her slippers and some books she wanted. I went back to the house to collect them. I made myself a cup of tea and sat drinking in Tom's kitchen. The phone rang. I decided not to answer it and let it ring. Then I changed my mind.

'Hello.'

'Is that you, Paul?'

'Yeah. Sheila?'

'Can you come and get me?'

'Come and get you?'

'Yes.'

'They've done it already?'

'No. They're not going to do it.'

'What are you talking about?'

'After you went the woman who does the operation came and saw me. Then she went away and the nurse came and told me to get dressed. She said it was too late.'

'Are you all right?'

'Yes. I want to come home.'

'Be right there.'

She sounded cheerful. I was nonplussed. When I went into

the ward she was laughingly distributing the fruit among the other women. I didn't drive straight home but took a detour through the countryside. We stopped at a village café for a cup of coffee and a cake. There was a holiday atmosphere. Sheila hadn't been so relaxed and chirpy since before Tom had asked me to leave their house. We drove onto the marshland and sat gazing across the maze of mud creek and marsh grass towards the sea. We held hands like young lovers and hardly spoke.

I wondered about Sheila's change of mood. I supposed she felt relieved at not having to go through with the abortion. And relief too that there were no choices any more. There was only one track now. She had to travel through the second half of her pregnancy to childbirth. And that must have seemed a safe distance off.

For myself, I felt weightless, as if the laws of nature no longer applied. Sheila was going to live with me. Then she wasn't. She was. She wasn't. She was. She wasn't. She was pregnant. She wasn't. She was. She wasn't. She was. She wanted to live with me, but living with me made her depressed. She was desperate for an abortion, but not having one made her happy. I'd fallen in love with someone who'd changed into somebody else. Did I still love her or didn't I? Did I still want to live with her, or had I just waded in too far ever to get out? Slowly it dawned on me that I was going to be a father for a second time, and I was not yet twenty-one. I'd stayed by Laura because she was pregnant. It had been a mistake. I was about to make the same mistake again, and there seemed no alternative.

I found it difficult to sleep that night. Dilemmas danced demoniacally through my mind. I decided to try to talk to Sheila, but next morning she had sunk into some deep place of despond far out of reach. She was still in bed when I arrived, and she stayed there for four weeks, alternately weeping and sleeping. I sat by her bed every day. The doctor prescribed ineffective pills for a fortnight and finally made an appointment for her to see a psychiatrist. That was the turning point. She made the effort to get up.

I drove her up the hill to the hospital and sat in the van while she was inside. I watched a gardener weeding among the shrubs at the side of the drive. He worked slowly and steadily, doubled over, shuffling forwards a step at a time. Every so often he'd straighten up, a hand on the small of his back. He was wearing old grey flannel trousers and a grey-striped flannelette collarless shirt and an ancient and greasy grey felt trilby. He looked like a figure out of the past, as if the world had accelerated away and left him behind, like a bus when the driver can't be bothered to wait for an old body to get to the bus stop.

I thought about my father. I had no memory of him, but I imagined he might have been like this man, bent over the earth and the life that grew in the earth. But he'd left all that, and died in the docks, lifting the dead weight of commerce in an alien place, shouldering the burden of another man's profit and being crushed under its weight. I began to daydream the dream of the landless man, of scrambling off the conveyor belt – out of the industrial waste. But I recognised that the romantic whim had no roots in a real world. My father spent his childhood in the stocks, unable to run free, unable to avoid what those bigoted and bitter people flung at him. And when he escaped, the world stretched him on its rack till his body broke. And maybe his spirit before that. Who knows?

40

I gazed at the old ⟨...⟩
on his back. Maybe h⟨...⟩
small backwater of peac⟨...⟩
I knew I couldn't grow i⟨...⟩
sort of job, bending to the ⟨...⟩
collecting mud till they grew ⟨...⟩
foot in front of the other.

The old man straightened up a⟨...⟩
small of his back, and tilted his hea⟨...⟩
sun shone on his tanned skin and his ⟨...⟩
off his hat with his free hand and wipe⟨...⟩
forehead. He put his hat back on and p⟨...⟩ ⟨...⟩
crown, and bent again to his work. I wonde⟨...⟩ ⟨...⟩t on,
what the hell he was doing there, creating flo⟨...⟩ around a
place like that, watching his work grow into ⟨...⟩e. And startlingly the van door was yanked open and Sheila got in quick
and angry, her mouth sewn into a tight seam. She didn't say
anything so I asked what had happened. She snorted.

I tried again. 'What did he say?'

'She's mad.'

'What?'

'She's mad.'

'Who's mad?'

'That woman.'

'What woman?'

'The psychiatrist.'

'The shrink was a woman?'

'Yes. She's mad.'

'What do you mean, she's mad?'

'I talked to her for ages about me and Tom and you. And you
know what she said?'

'What she say?'

'Do you know what her solution to the problem was?'

'No.'

'Guess.'

'I can't. I dunno. What?'

'She said Tom and I ought to have a baby.'

'What!'

'Yes.'

'You what!'

... closer together.'

... she know?'

...s. Said to get rid of it or have it adopted or something.
Then to start afresh with Tom and have a baby.'

'Didn't you tell her how you felt about Tom?'

'Yes. She said I'd feel different if I had his baby.'

'And what about the baby? Didn't she think about that?
Didn't she think about whether the kid would want to be born
into a dead bloody marriage?'

'I told you, she's mad.'

'You're not kidding she's fucking mad. Fucking irrespons-
ible. She really said that?'

'Yes.'

'Might as well have written to bleeding Evelyn Home.'

'Yes.'

'She gets paid all that to sit there and fuck people up? What
did you say?'

'I said she was mad.'

'What did she say?'

'She said, *Look, my dear, I'm here to help you.*'

We both laughed. It was the first time Sheila had laughed for
a month. 'You're coming away with me,' I said.

She stopped laughing. 'What on earth are you talking
about?'

'You're coming with me. All this coming and going's
finished. We're going to make a new start.'

'Are you serious?'

'I'm serious,' I said. 'I'm serious.'

Finally I had made the decision for Sheila that she'd been unable to make. I took her back to the caravan. The first week we stayed in bed most of the time, kissing, caressing, exploring. When she touched my legs and feet, the skin of them told me they'd never been lovingly touched before. It felt as though my skin was crying out for more, reaching out to her soothing hands, the way the hairs of your body will reach out to the magnetism of static electricity. It was as if her hands were spreading balm on wounds. Sheila said that week was like being brought gently back to life after dying. Like being warmed slowly through after months in the deep freeze.

We had a few good weeks. The site was being closed to make way for a new road. Ours was the last caravan there. As the other people and vans left, the countryside was reclaiming its own. The whole site was our private garden where wild flowering weeds ran rampant about the place. When the weather was fine we would wash under the willow tree and eat our food squeezed close together on the door step. We walked a lot in the surrounding lanes. Sheila knew the names of wild flowers and trees. The hedgerows were rich in plants I'd never noticed. 'This is hazel,' she'd say. 'The nuts will be ready in another month or so. There's lots this year. There's going to be lots of blackberries too. This is wild strawberry. It has little tiny fruits, but they're lovely and sweet. That's golden rod. And look at all the rose hips. I should collect them and make syrup.' She gathered armfuls of flowers and small branches and stood them around in jam jars and milk bottles and made the caravan into a home.

But she became increasingly irritable. She wasn't sleeping well. She kept dreaming about giving birth to non-human things, and waking up distraught. She became more and more unreasonable. She got hysterical one evening when I came

43

home late. I'd had to walk four miles because my old van had finally given up the ghost. I reacted by shouting and swearing at her before I remembered what she was going through, that there was probably something deformed inside her, feeding off her. Some grotesque parasite. Secretly I hoped it would die, but it was very much alive. And kicking. There was not much joy in seeing it kick when you feared it was maybe kicking without feet.

As the birth crept towards us, so did the date we had to be off the caravan site. I kept telling her that I would find somewhere – that I wasn't going to let her give birth in the street. I constantly tried to reassure her that the baby would be all right.

'If it hasn't been deformed by rubella,' she sobbed, 'half of it probably got washed out with the bleeding.'

''Course it didn't. Your body knows best. Better than any bloody doctor or rubella society. If there was something wrong with it your body would've rejected it, would have thrown it out. That's what miscarriages are for.'

'Then how do you think so many deformed children are born?'

'How do I think so many deformed . . . how do I think . . . you want to know . . . you want to know why . . .' frantically fumbling through the recesses of my mind for something reasonable and reassuring to say. 'Well, I'll tell you why . . . I'll tell you. Listen. If a woman's in danger of losing the baby, what do they do? They coddle her, don't they? Make her rest. They stuff her with drugs. Look at Bud's wife. Made her stay in bed. She wasn't allowed to get up for weeks. But she lost it anyway. She was lucky. The unlucky ones are the ones when they save it. The woman's body's seen it was a reject. Right? So it wants to throw it back. Then they stop it. They plug her up so it can't get out. Don't they? Put a cork in.' She smiled. She was sitting on the edge of the bed. I was on my knees in front of her, looking up at her, holding her hands, worshipping her. 'That's what they do. Straight up. They put the plug straight up. They lay her down and dope her up. Don't let her carry on naturally. Bud's wife felt fine. Wanted to get up and do things. But the old sawbones said no. Thought he knew better then her own body. If she'd got up she'd have thrown it out in a day or two. But what happened? She lay there in bed dribbling blood onto the

45

sheets for two weeks. More than two weeks. But she lost it in the end anyway. Your body knows best.'

'Does it?'

''Course it does. Your body knows. And look at all these drugs and things they give people. That can't be natural, can it? It's not natural to have all these drugs and everything. That's how they fuck up these kids. They don't know half what some of these things can cause. But you're not having none of that, because, first you didn't think you were pregnant, and then you wanted to get rid of it anyway. And now you won't go near a quack because of how they've been. So you've had none of that. Not only did nobody stop you from miscarrying, but you would've done it if you could. And you couldn't. So it must be all right. Mustn't it? Ay?'

'I don't know.'

''Course you know. You feel fine, don't you? Physically I mean. Look at you. Radiant like a bride, you are. Fit as a fiddle. Your tits are getting bigger every day.' I pushed her knees apart and thrust myself forward between her thighs. She held my head against her breasts with both hands.

'But what about all that bleeding?'

'Clearing out, gel. Clearing out. If you've got a house, and a friend's coming to stay, you clear out the spare room and make it nice for them, don't you?'

'And what are *we* going to do about a house?'

'Well, no need to worry about that. That's just a sort of . . . you know . . . material problem. You can always sort them out one way or the other. The important problems are the inside ones. Like our little problem in there.' I slid my face down onto her tight belly. 'Oi, you! Wotcha, cock. I'm talking about you. Do you know what? You're a right little problem, you are. What's that you say? Tell her what? Tell Sheila to get stuffed? Don't be daft. That's what caused all the trouble in the first place.'

Sheila was laughing. I couldn't see her face or hear her, but I could feel her laughter through her body. I brought my head up and nestled it into her swelling breasts. 'The other problems are the real ones, love. We'll find a place to live. As long as we've got each other everything'll be all right. We can always find somewhere.'

46

'The eternal optimist.' She was more cheerful now.

'It's not optimism. It's common sense. Everything's going to be all right.'

'Is it reasonable to expect the sun to rise tomorrow?'

'What?'

'Philosophical question. I had it in an exam at college. Is it reasonable to expect the sun to rise tomorrow?'

I sat back on my haunches. 'So long as it ain't too cloudy.'

'No. Behind the clouds.'

''Course it is.'

'Why is it?'

'Why is it what?'

'Reasonable.'

'What a load of old cobblers. How much do philosophers get paid a week?'

'More than we do.'

'I wouldn't begrudge anyone that. Even a philosopher.'

'What are you going to do, Paul?' Her tone had changed. Flowers to briars.

'What am *I* going to do?'

'Yes. When the baby's born.'

'I'm going to help look after it.'

'Aren't you going to get a job or anything?'

'Get a job? You were always on about Tom because he wouldn't stay at home.'

'Yes, but it's different.'

'What do I want a job for? I mean, if I was working I wouldn't be able to look after you, would I?'

'I'm glad you're not working now. But I mean after.'

'You mean once you've had the kid you won't need me any more?'

'No. I don't mean that.'

'Well, the kid'll need me. I'm its father, aren't I? Well, am I?'

'Don't be silly.'

'OK, if I'm its father, I'll need to look after it.'

'But we can't go on living on state welfare the rest of our lives.'

'Why not?'

'I just wouldn't like to, that's all.'

'Well, if you're so keen, you get a job and I'll look after the baby.'

47

'Do we have to be poor and homeless always?'

'Yeah. Yeah, we do. You can have a taste of what it's like. I've always been poor and fucking homeless. I don't give a toss about that, but also I never had anyone who gave a fish's tit about me. You know that? That's what I care about. My kid's not going to grow up like that. They already took my first baby away. Well, no bastard's going to take this one. Unless it's a bleeding mutation or something, and then I'll take care of it with my own fucking hands. I won't let it live. I tell you that. I'll save it that fucking misery at any rate. But if it's all right, I'm its father, and it'll grow up knowing there's someone in the world that cares about it and loves it.'

Her voice was cold and quiet, cutting and calm. 'What about me? Are you saying I won't be able to care for and love my own child?'

I leaned forward, my finger jutting towards her face. 'I don't give a fuck about you, whether you love it or not. That's up to you. That's nothing to do with me. I'm just telling you, no one's taking my kid away from me. And if that means Lady Never-shit's got to live in a style to which she ain't fucking accustomed, that's too fucking bad. You've always had plenty. It won't do you no bloody harm to see how the other half lives.'

Her cry was more like the scream of an industrial saw tearing its way through steel. It went on and on. I sank back onto my heels, horrified at the ugliness of her face and body as she cringed away from me, and I thought, *Oh, Jesus fucking Christ, what have I done now?*

When I was a kid my mother used to have continual outbursts of irrational temper. She would bellow like a bull elephant, fulminate with frustration, and sob with self-pity. Sometimes she would put a cushion in the gas oven for her head and, kneeling in front of it, turn on the taps. These fits and the accompanying physical assaults on me seemed usually to have little reason, and sometimes no reason at all. I've learned since that there is a reason for everything, but the reasons then were often nothing to do with me. She'd been brutalised from birth to motherhood. I once saw an American serviceman rip her blouse open in the street in front of his friends and I was ashamed because her brassiere was grubby. She was unloved and lonely and living in poverty. She worked long hours in an oppressive factory for a pittance, and came home to a depressing room and an unwelcome responsibility.

Because of my mother's yelling and my yowling we were turned out of our bedsitting room. We hired a handcart and trundled our belongings through the back doubles to another grim terraced house in another grimy street. There, we had two upstairs rooms. One we used as a bedroom, the other as a living room. To get to the kitchen we went down unlit stairs and through the room where the old lady who owned the house was always slumped like a heap of jumble in an armchair in the corner. She smelt as if she was already dead. To get to the lavatory we went through the kitchen into the back yard.

The neighbourhood was rough. I wasn't allowed to play out. Because my mother had been a servant to the aristocracy she thought we were superior to our neighbours. (She kept a scrapbook of the Royal Family, cutting pictures out of the *Daily Mirror* and *Woman's Weekly*.) I had jobs to do after school and at weekends, but sometimes I used to sneak out in the holidays.

The old cadaver downstairs had enough life left in her to inform on me when I did.

'Have you been out?'

'No.'

'No, what?'

'No, Mum.'

'I want the truth. Have you been out running the streets?'

'No.'

'Don't lie to me. How many times do I have to tell you? I'm your mother. I can always tell when you're lying. Have you been out? Look at me when I'm speaking to you. Now answer me. Have you been out?'

I glanced up into her eyes which tried to hold mine like talons. Tore myself away like tearing my skin off brambles.

'Answer me!'

I was shrinking, making my way into that secret place. My skin was becoming leathery and the leather was changing to scales and the scales to armour. I was dying slowly. Feeling was draining like fluid from my body so that I would feel less pain. She spoke staccato through gritted teeth. The words separated, isolated.

'Will – you – answer me – when – I speak – to you!'

A series of replies bobbed through my brain like a fleet of bits of rubbish in a brook. *Yes, I have been out . . . I can go out if I like . . . Why shouldn't I . . . What's it got to do with you . . . Mind your own business . . . If you know why ask . . . Drop dead.* But I stood as immobile and silent as a ceremonial guard at a cenotaph.

'Go and fetch me a coathanger!'

I moved as if by remote control. I gave up the robot to her authority but kept myself to myself. I went into the bedroom. There was a chest of drawers in front of the window, and the wardrobe stood facing it between two single iron beds. I opened the wardrobe door and stood on the floor of the wardrobe so that I could reach. I slipped one of her cheap cotton dresses off its coathanger and laid it carefully on the bed so that it wouldn't crease. I carried the coathanger into the other room. She stood where I'd left her. The skin of her face was taut and drained of colour. A slight trembling of her hands was the only evidence that she was not a waxwork.

'Come here!' She pointed to a place on the lino a foot in front

50

of her. I edged forward. 'Here, I said!' Her voice was harsh, grating like metal on metal in a road accident. I shuffled forward again like a camp internee in a gas chamber queue. 'Here!' I stepped onto a red diamond in a brown circle in a yellow square on the cold and ugly lino. It was like stepping onto a trapdoor with the rope around my neck. I placed my body like a dead fish on a fishmonger's slab. She took the coathanger and pointed it at me like a gutting knife. 'Now, I want the truth.'

The one thing she couldn't stand above all else was not being able to reach. Not being able to force a submission. 'Have you been out?' I stared at a brown button on a fawn cardigan. 'Will you look at me? How many times do I have to tell you!' I glanced at her face. The hatred which disfigured it stabbed at me like a blunt sword. 'Have you been out? Answer me! You will answer me if I have to beat you black and blue. I mean it! You will *not* defy me!'

Explosion. Tension released in an orgy of thrashing and tears. Eventually she would tire, unable to go on, hating herself for what her frustration was making her do to that poor helpless little bastard I used to be. My wailing must have wrenched at her like an abortion. 'Stop that crying! Stop that noise! Or do you want another one! What are the neighbours going to think! Stop it! Stop it!' And the bashing would go on till the bawling was forced underground and battened down.

'Get your coat on. I'm going to get the children's home to come and take you away. You stand outside the front door and wait till they come. And don't you dare move an inch!'

It was good to be out of her reach. The winter wind was warm by comparison. But I felt like a fox facing hounds on a cliff top. I stood transfixed, not wanting to stay, nor to go back to the home. My infertile imagination could conjure up no other alternative.

It was during the time Sheila was waiting to go into hospital for the abortion that I had my only liaison with a woman which I remember as wholly warm. I used to spend the days with Sheila. Evenings, I was at a loose end. I've always experienced being alone as unbearable pain. One evening I drove out in my van as desperate for a woman's company as a junkie for a fix. I parked outside a village pub. The bar was as small as a front parlour and there were no vacant seats. I carried my drink through a doorway to an adjoining room. It was larger, with tables and chairs scattered around the floor area and benches around the walls. I no sooner entered than I realised I'd made a mistake. A man was on his feet reading from a sheet of paper in his hand. I tried to withdraw but a woman sitting on a bench just inside the door held my arm. 'Stay,' she whispered. The people in the room broke into applause and the reader sat down. 'It's a poetry reading,' she said. 'You're welcome.' The people on the bench shuffled along to make room for me.

It was hot in there and the smoke stung my eyes. I sat, not to hear the poems, but to be close to the woman.

An elderly lady stood up and began to read, in a nasal sing-song, rhyming drivel about silver moonlight on the sea shore. I watched the woman beside me. She was maybe ten years older than me – in her late twenties. She had naturally blonde curly hair, pale blue eyes and a small mouth. The only make-up she wore was on her eyelashes. Her eyes were on the reader but she didn't appear to be listening. She was locked in a misery of her own. My arm was against her arm. My leg against her leg. Her warmth came through to me. The contact was like alcohol to an alcoholic.

When it was her turn she read a poem about horses that had broken through a fence and trampled a garden she had made.

There was a break for replenishing glasses. I bought her a

52

drink and brought it to her. 'What do you think of the poems?' she said.

'I don't know anything about poetry.'

'You don't need to know anything to know whether you like the poems or not.'

'I thought they were a load of rubbish. Except yours. Yours was the only one that was about anything. I think if you open your mouth to say something you should have something worth saying. Otherwise keep your trap shut.'

She looked surprised. 'What was mine about, then?'

'Your marriage – not working.'

'How did you know that?'

'Your poem. Your face.'

'My face?'

'You look as though you've cried yourself to sleep every night for a year.'

She looked at me quizzically, and slowly shook her head. Then a chubby, cheery man was on his feet calling for quiet. I pressed myself against the woman with my mind closed and drank in the comfort of her body.

Her second poem was about an autistic child. The child played in a closed world while specialists pontificated in a closed room.

At the end of the reading she bought me a drink. Most of the poetry people left. A few clusters collected around tables talking noisily. She sat close to me. 'Well?' she said, raising her eyebrows.

'I never thought about autistic kids before. It made me think. I've been thinking about your first poem too. There's something wrong with it.'

'How do you mean?'

'That horse business really happened, didn't it?'

'Yes.'

'You were upset by the horse trampling on your flowers. It seemed like the way you'd worked so hard to cultivate your marriage, and now all the love seems to have been trampled on.'

'Well, it seems to have communicated to you all right.'

'But it's not right.'

'Why not?'

53

'It wasn't some force from outside that broke in and spoiled things. The soil was diseased. That's why the marriage died.'

She sipped at her beer thoughtfully. Then she put her glass down and looked at me. 'You're right.' she said. 'That's very helpful.'

I felt embarrassed and looked away. 'If I can help somebody . . .' I said.

'You really are an amazing young man,' she said. And suddenly I felt hot with anger.

'Don't patronise me,' I snapped. 'You think people like me – working-class yobbos – are all halfwits.'

The publican called time. A pot boy tried to take my glass but I held on to it. 'No, I don't,' she said. 'Really I don't.' She put her hand on mine. Her skin was smooth and her touch gentle. 'My husband's a doctor. I'm a social worker. Our friends are professional people. But I don't think any of them realise what state our marriage is in. None of my family seem to be aware of how unhappy I am. I don't think anybody here understood my poem. It's nothing to do with class.'

I drained my glass. 'Can I give you a lift home?' I said.

'Thank you. That would be nice. But I've got my own car.' She smiled apologetically.

'Then perhaps you could give me a lift home.'

'What about your car?'

'I haven't got a car. I was going to nick one,' I lied.

She looked shocked, unsure. 'You'd better not do *that*.'

It was cool in the caravan. I'd left the bed down. Just in case. She sat on the side of it. 'Let me take your coat,' I said. 'It'll soon warm up.'

I made coffee and sat beside her. I sipped at the hot liquid and then put my mug on the floor. She held onto hers with both hands until I took it away. I began to kiss her. Every so often she twisted her face away from me, but each time she allowed me to turn it back until my lips joined with hers. I laid her back across the bed. Soon she struggled to sit up. 'This is a bit of a surprise,' she said.

'But it's a nice surprise,' I said.

'I'm married.'

'In a manner of speaking.'

54

'Don't you have ... anybody?'

'Sort of.'

I kissed her, and in kissing her let my weight press her down again. I could feel the conflict within her. She struggled up. 'I'm not sure about this,' she said. 'And what about your ... sort of?'

'We're not taking anything away from anybody else by giving something to each other.'

'I don't know.'

'You must know. You must have had the experience of loving somebody and feeling warmth towards someone else.'

'But our way of being brought up makes us need exclusive relationships.'

'This evening we can make love exclusively to each other.'

Again I tipped her back and we kissed and again she sat up. 'Oh dear,' she said. 'I don't like this role. But I'm not sure.'

'I want to tell you something.' I pushed her back down onto the bed and held her there, but raised myself so that I could look into her eyes. 'In the first place I invited you back because you're pretty and you've got a nice body. But I find myself liking you more and more. I think you're a lovely *person*.'

'That's the nicest thing anybody's said to me for a very long time. But you don't know me.'

'I do. I think you can know someone very well when you first meet them. A year later you can support what you think of them with evidence from what you've heard them say or seen them do. But how often do you find someone's not what you thought they were?'

'You're probably right.'

'And I know that you're a very lovely lady.'

Again I kissed her, and while she responded to the demands of my mouth I slipped my arm behind her knees and lifted her completely onto the bed. She pushed against my hand but not strongly enough to prevent me from lifting her bra over her breasts. I fondled them and kissed them. But soon she sat up again. 'What are you bobbing up for now?' I said.

'I can't make love with you,' she said. 'I'm not on the pill.'

'What do you do with your husband?'

'We haven't done anything for two years.'

'Two years! I can't believe that. How do you survive?'

55

She peered into the gloom of the tin-can living-cum-bedroom before she answered. 'I've got used to the idea of being alone. I've begun to think that I won't ever be able to love anyone again.'

'That's nonsense. You've got lots of love in you. You're like an empty house now with wooden boards nailed across the doors and windows to keep people out. You've got to take down those shutters. Let the sun shine in. Let people in. You're bound to find one you can love.'

We laid down again and I pressed her to me. 'You're strong,' she said. 'I like that.'

'You need lots of cuddling,' I said. 'Does your husband never cuddle you?'

'He never touches me.'

'Everyone needs to be cuddled.'

'Sex has never been any good with him. I got married before I slept with him. I suppose that was silly.'

'Yeah. Very.'

'It seemed a sensible marriage. Like my parents'. Theirs was a marriage of convenience. Actually I fell in love with someone else just before the wedding.'

'And you still went ahead?'

'Yes.'

'Well, that was *really* silly.'

'It's ridiculous, isn't it? My husband and I, in our professional capacities, are advising other people on their marital problems and we can't even talk about our own. We separated after a year. I had two boyfriends and sex was fine with them. Then I went back with Julian. I got pregnant and had a miscarriage.'

'Thank Christ for that.'

'And he's never touched me since.'

'You need to find someone who wants to touch you all the time. Someone who lusts after you.'

We began to kiss each other wildly as though we were trying to condense two years' passion into ten minutes. I rolled on top of her and she opened her legs to accept me between her thighs. Then she stopped me again. It was like riding a big dipper. 'I don't want to be in this position,' she said.

'That's OK,' I said. 'We'll do it in any position you like.'

'I asked for that. I mean I don't want to keep saying no all the time.'

'The answer to that little problem's easy. Just say, yes, yes, yes, yes.'

'But I'm still unsure, and it's not fair on either of us. I want to think about it. I don't want to be hurried.'

'You should go on the pill.'

'There hasn't seemed any point.'

'You never know when you might need it. You don't want to waste an opportunity. You might go out tomorrow and meet someone marvellous.'

'I suppose so.'

'When's your period?'

'Soon. A few days.'

'Well, it'd be safe now.'

'You can't rely on that.'

'Some people go through their married lives relying on nothing else.'

'I'll start the pill after my period.'

'Then you'll meet me again?'

'Yes. But it's not safe straight away.'

'I'll meet you in a few weeks.'

'All right.'

'Four weeks tonight – at that pub.'

'All right.'

'And we'll make love then?'

'Probably. It'll give me time to think about it. But you're so much younger than me.'

'I don't see why that should matter.'

'I suppose not.'

We lay in each other's arms, sharing our warmth. I could see through the caravan window a three-quarter white moon, swollen like a pregnant womb. Its roundness gave me pleasure and comfort, like the roundness of the woman under me.

'I've thought of a reason,' she said, 'why I may say no. We might be opening ourselves to too much hurt.'

'I knew an old lady,' I said, 'who gave me some advice. She said she'd always been taught to say no, and she always did say no. And all she had to show for it was thirty years of wasted life with a man she didn't want, and following that, twenty

57

widowed years of loneliness. She said to me, take the advice of an old woman who knows. Never say no. Say yes. To everything.'

'Sounds like good advice.'

'So say yes. Take down the boards. Let the sun shine in. Let me come in. I want to come in you.'

'Not now.'

'When?'

'Next time. I want to go now.'

We stood up. She arranged her clothes and pressed her fingers lightly into her hair. 'Look at the moon when you go out,' I said. 'It'll look exactly the same.'

I put my arms round her and kissed her. Then she said, 'I suppose it's a trite thing to say, but it feels so natural being with you.'

'I don't think it's trite at all. I feel at ease with you too.' We lingered, kissing, in the narrow space between bed and cupboard, alternately passionate and gentle. 'I don't want you to go,' I said.

'I don't want to go,' she said. 'That scares me.'

But she did go. I never saw her again. I don't know her name. Or where she lives. I only know that sometimes, when I've been numb, I've remembered her, and the memory has brought me warmth and enough light to see a little way ahead. But now, even that small flame has died.

Sheila and I clung on in the caravan as long as we could, but finally autumn came, as boisterous as a bailiff. We didn't wait to witness the caravan being towed away. The earth-moving machines were noisily at work from early morning, and this fuelled my fantasy in which a bulldozer would mash our home into matchwood. We took only what we could carry. Because Sheila was so obviously pregnant I had been unable to find anywhere for us to go. I'd tried house agents, the local paper, sweet shop windows, without success. The only person I could think of who might help was my old school mate, Bud. He was working for a big construction company up north, building a motorway. He lived in a trailer on site. I didn't have enough money for the train so we travelled by coach. Sheila found the journey uncomfortable and exhausting. It was nearly midnight when we arrived. There were no taxis at the bus station, and hardly any people in the streets. Instead of being built of brick, all the buildings were of stone. It was a pleasant evening and the place had a foreign feel about it. I half expected the townsfolk to talk in some unintelligible tongue. After being given directions and told emphatically it was too far to walk we set out on foot. Sheila·didn't complain but lumbered so slowly and gracelessly behind me, her silent tears shining on her cheeks in the light from the street lamps, that I wanted to hit her. My arms felt as if they were being drawn out into stringy lengths, like chewing gum, by the weight of the cases.

'Everything's going to be all right,' I said gently, urging her on. 'This is a new chapter – a new life. It's a good time to start fresh, with the baby due. This is a new beginning. We can leave all the shit behind us and start a new day. Come on, love.' She forced a smile to humour me and the rage seethed in me like sea fermenting among rocks at high tide.

After walking for half an hour at a pace slower than that of a geriatric snail we came to a long terraced row which contained an unoccupied house that was being modernised. There was a new pink wooden frame in the front, but no glass in the window. 'Hey, look. We can stay the night here. We'll find Bud in the morning.'

'How can we?'

'How can we what?'

'Stay here?'

'What do you mean, how can we? We just do, that's all.'

I stepped over the low garden wall, threw the bags through the window and climbed into the room. I groped my way back along the dark hall and opened the front door. 'Come on.'

She came reluctantly through the gateway. 'Are you sure it'll be all right?'

''Course it will. Come on, for Christ's sake. Here, wait a minute. As it's our new home I ought to carry you over the threshold.'

'Don't. Stop it.' I tried to lift her but she pushed me away crossly as if I was an old drunk trying to interfere with her in an alley. I felt a strong urge to punch her again. I followed her into the hall and closed the door. 'It's dark,' she said.

''Course it's fucking dark.'

'Shall I see if the lights work?'

'Don't be daft.'

'Why?'

'Well, it's an empty house.'

'But you said it was all right.'

'Well of course it fucking is – but we don't want to attract attention, do we?'

I edged around her and went upstairs. The front bedroom had glass in the window and was gently lit by an orange street light. 'Come up here,' I called. The new floorboards looked as white as a wedding gown. It was mild for October and the room was surprisingly warm and cosy. I could hear Sheila cumbrously climbing the stairs.

'This is great,' I said. 'I told you our luck was changing. A place like this would do us fine, wouldn't it?' I went out onto the landing. I kissed Sheila on the forehead as I squeezed past her. 'In there. Best bedroom.' I went down a step and into a small bathroom which housed a new blue bath, basin and bog. I thought *if the bog's working, the baby will be all right*. I tried the flush. Water rushed into the bowl with a roar and the floating dog-ends and dirt disappeared. I felt as perky as a kid at a pantomime.

I made a mattress by tipping our clothes out of our suitcases and we spent a reasonably comfortable night on the floor. I woke several times feeling cold. I kept intending to get up and jump around to warm up but never managed it before I slithered back down a slippery slope into sleep. I dreamt I was a prisoner. I was in a foetus position, inside a box so small I couldn't move. It was agony – the wanting to move and not being able to. The only part of me I could move was my arms. I reached painstakingly round my body, persevering until I was hugging myself, my hands on my back. I couldn't make out what it was I could feel. It was like one of those party games when you're blindfolded and given something to touch and you have to guess what it is. I was incarcerated, screwed up inside this little box, hugging myself. My hands crawled over my back. And what I could feel was maggots. A seething writhing mass of soft white maggots. I was decaying, and I was being eaten alive.

I woke feeling sick and afraid. I called Sheila but she didn't respond. I shook her shoulder. 'Sheila.'

'Mm.'

'Sheila.'

'Mm.'

'I just had this dream.'

Her breathing went on heavy and uninterrupted. I cried quietly. I don't know why. After a while I went back to sleep. I was woken again by the heavy drone of early morning traffic. I was stiff and my hip bones were sore. I went quietly into the bathroom, had a slash and splashed cold water into my face. In the back room downstairs, among the ladders and paint pots and planks, I found an electric kettle and all the necessaries for a brew. I couldn't believe my luck. I made two mugs of tea and took them upstairs.

It wasn't yet fully light when we left the house. We thumbed a lift up to the site from a bloke on his way to work who pointed out Bud's caravan. Bud opened the door to my knock without having to move away from the tiny grill where, with his mouth

61

already full, he was making more toast. He looked astonished, and then delighted, his eyes narrowed to slits by his toothy grin. He flapped his hand at us to invite us in and we squeezed past him. Anne sat up blearily in bed. She smiled and greeted us, but her eyes said, *What the hell are you doing here? Clear off out of it!*

I told Bud why we were there while he stuffed folded toast into his mouth and washed it down with swigs of tea. 'You can stay here till you get fixed up,' he said.

'Where can they sleep?' Anne objected.

'On the beds, dummy. Where else would they sleep – on the draining board? Those two seats make into single beds,' he said to me. 'I've got to go. I'm late again.' He grabbed a donkey jacket and nodded to me to go outside with him. 'Got any lolly?' he asked.

'Nah. Not a penny. Used it all to get here.'

'Don't say anything to her.' He handed me a couple of quid and ran off across the churned-up mud. 'See you later,' he called.

Sheila stayed at the caravan with Anne while I went into town and signed on at the labour exchange. I wasn't entitled to benefit so I asked for directions to the welfare office. The room there was grey with smoke and smelt of stale piss. We sat in rows as if we were in a cinema, facing a screen on the wall in front of us. It said: THE NEAREST PUBLIC CONVENIENCES ARE IN MARKET SQUARE.

Across the aisle from me sat a short, dumpy young woman who had a baby face and big breasts. She had a boy and a girl with her, aged about four and three. Whenever she noticed me fondling her body with my eyes she blushed and began to talk to the children. The kids sat passively at first but gradually became restless. And I became restless with them. Unlike the kids I couldn't let off steam by hopping around. I tried to damp down the flames of my anger, but it smouldered more and more fiercely as time went on. After we'd been there nearly two hours the kids were running up and down the space in front of the seats shouting and laughing. An old clerk with a yellow-stained white moustache peered out belligerently from behind the reception desk. He looked like a retired army sergeant. Suddenly he began to bellow as if he thought he was still on the parade ground. 'Can't you keep those children quiet!'

The young mother with the heavy breasts that I wanted to push my face into, coloured with shame. She leaned forward and called in a hushed and urgent voice, 'John! Christine!'

'That's all right, gel,' I said to her in a voice loud enough for the clerk to hear. 'You leave them alone. They're all right. They're alive, that's all. These corpses that work in here can't bear to see anybody living. They're non-human. They're bleeding zombies – dead from the toenails up.' I pointed at the reception clerk. It was his turn to go red. 'You know what they want to do, don't you? Kill anything that moves. Stamp out any

63

spark of life they see.' I turned to the audience sitting patiently in rows around me. 'That's why they keep us sitting here for hours on end. It's not necessary. They just do it so you have to sit here and clench up and crush out any feelings you've got in you so you're docile when you reach the grille. They're like these bleeding old spinster school teachers who work off all their nasty jealous little feelings on the kids. They're like ghouls waltzing round a battlefield with a pistol after the big guns have stopped. They go trip-tripping around the bodies looking for movement, for any sign of life. And if they see it, they put their pistol to the person's head, lick their chops, and blow half his face off. And then they smile and drool and walk on. It's the only pleasure they're capable of.'

Apart from a baby somewhere at the back snivelling there was silence in the room. The waiting people lowered their eyes in embarrassment and studied their knees or feet, or the dog-ends on the dirty floor. The clerk wrote something down on a memo pad. Then he got up, scraping his chair on the floor, and went out. I looked at the young mother and felt myself blush. The two kids were standing against her, staring at me with big eyes. 'Don't you take any notice of them, gel,' I said softly. 'Kids should be running and playing. Well, am I right or am I right?' I asked the room in general. No one answered. 'Go on, kids,' I said. 'You don't want to take any notice of that old git. You go and enjoy yourselves.' They pressed closer to their mother, holding onto her skirt and coat.

Over the loudspeaker a metallic voice startled me with my name. 'Paul Greig. Cubicle four.'

I went through a sliding door and found an unnumbered row of horse-boxes. It was all part of their psychological game. They fucked you about as much as they could. They kept you waiting for hours on end. They made you uneasy and afraid of doing the wrong thing. They were aloof and uninformative. In the end they got you feeling like a bug that had just crawled out from under the carpet so you'd be glad to accept whatever they gave you, even if it was less then you were entitled to. You'd take it and get out, and in future prefer to go without rather than go through it all again. I stayed where I was, staring over the top of the partitions, until a clerk's head bobbed into view.

'Mr Greig?'

'Yeah.'

'In here, please.'

The man behind the counter was an old, spare thirty. He was tidy and grey, and wore rimless glasses. He started the long rigmarole of questions and form filling. Name? Place of birth? Colour of your grandma's knickers?

'Why did you move?' he asked when the forms were duly filled.

'I told you. Couldn't find a job or a place to live.'

'Why don't you go to London?'

'Because there's nowhere to live in London.'

'Big cities are the places to find work.'

'But not the places to find accommodation.'

'There's unemployment here.'

'There's unemployment everywhere. It's government policy.'

'Don't you think it was unwise to come here without finding a job first?'

'Don't you think it was unwise to stay where I was without anywhere to live?'

'What prospects have you for finding employment?'

'I only arrived here last night. And anyway, I've been through all this at the dole office. It's their job to help me find work – not yours. You've got a B1 there which is proof that I'm signed on as being available and willing to work.'

'Yes, Mr Greig, but . . .'

'And I've come here because I need an emergency payment.'

He compressed his pale, mean lips tightly together and glared angrily at me through his glasses. I perched on the front edge of my metal chair leaning forward towards him. 'If I'd stayed where I was, I'd've been paid this morning. As it is I've got no money. My wife's eight months pregnant.'

'I thought we'd ascertained that you weren't married.'

'My common law wife is eight months pregnant. We're homeless and penniless.'

'But you've given me this address . . .'

'I've given you the address of where we're staying.'

'Well, let me get down the particulars about that.'

I took a deep breath to help me hold down the desire to grab him by the lapels of his shoddy grey jacket, haul him across the counter and nut him between the eyes. I sat back a little on the chair to make sure he was out of reach of my hands.

'Now this address you've given me – you say it's a caravan?'

'A friend's caravan.'

'May I see your rent book?'

'I haven't got a rent book. We're just staying ...'

'How much rent do you pay?'

I sighed, trying to speak quietly. 'I keep telling you, we're staying temporarily with friends and we don't pay any rent.'

'Then you haven't got a rent book.'

'We haven't got a rent book.'

He looked more collected again. Almost pleased. 'Well, I'm sorry, Mr Greig. Very sorry. But unless you can produce a rent book, we can't make a payment.'

'What are you talking about – what's a rent book got to do with it?'

'It's the regulations, Mr Greig. I'm sorry. I don't make the regulations, but I am bound by them.'

'That's what they used to say when they shovelled the Jews into the fucking gas chambers.'

'I will not be sworn at. If you use that language again I'll call the police.' His voice rose, shrill as a eunuch's. His hands gripped the edge of the counter. For a moment I felt sorry for him. I imagined him going home to a nagging old widowed mother who packed him up spam sandwiches, and made him go to chapel, and polish his shoes, and be in by ten. And his only escape from having her claw and paw at him with her dissatisfaction and loneliness was sitting in this dingy office like a prisoner who'd been made prison librarian, being visited day after day by a succession of the subdued or belligerent downtrodden.

'I'm sorry,' I said. He sank back like a soufflé that's been taken out of the oven too soon. 'I realise it's not your fault. This must be a bloody awful job.'

He rose up again several inches off his chair. 'I won't have it. I will not tolerate this language.'

I really did want to hit him then. But I bit back my words and clenched my teeth till he slowly subsided once more. We glowered at each other for a while like boxers in our corners between rounds. The counter stood between us like a class barrier.

'I can't make you a payment unless you produce a rent book.'

'Look, I'm not paying rent, but I still need to eat, don't I?'

'Well, I suggest you find some accommodation, get a rent book, and then come back to see us again.'

'If we haven't starved to death in the meantime. And how am I supposed to get somewhere to live without any money? You know as well as I do, you have to pay rent in advance. If you won't give me any money I can't get anywhere to live. If I can't get anywhere to live you won't give me any money. That's great, that is. And in the meantime my wife . . . my common law wife, is getting nearer to having a baby and's getting no nourishment. If she dies, or the baby dies, it'll be blood on your hands.'

He collected his papers and stood up. 'Perhaps Mrs Hill would be better advised to go back to her husband.' He turned and walked out of sight leaving me with a fantasy of vaulting the counter and going after him. I imagined holding him by the hair and smashing his face against the wall until it was pulped and juicy as a ripe melon. I got to my feet empty-handed and trembling with impotent rage.

In secondary school I was undersized and skinny. I was bullied by bigger boys. Picked on by prefects. Tormented by teachers. Lines. Detention. Sarcasm. Slaps. The slipper. The cane. Punished for being late. For not wearing cap or uniform. For not doing homework. For not paying attention. For insolence by look, or by silence. For disobedience. For fighting. For skiving in the bogs. For playing hookey. It was like stumbling through a maze of distorting mirrors that had no way out.

There really is a them and an us. But it's not the rich against the poor. It's the zombies against the normals. The lawkeepers against the freemen. You find *them* everywhere, in all sorts of uniforms: park-keepers, policemen, prefects, petty bureaucrats, prison officers, and of course, pathetic teachers.

'**W**hat are you doing, boy?' I pulled myself through the window and stood in the classroom. 'Speak up, boy. I'm talking to you. What do you think you're doing?'

I looked disdainfully at his indignant face. He was a self-righteous little man with long hair growing out of his nostrils. His shabby suit was powdered with chalk. *Ask a silly question and you deserve a silly answer*, I thought to myself. But I decided against giving one. 'Climbing in the window.'

'Climbing in the window, what?'

Climbing in the window, you bloody halfwit, I thought. But I said nothing. I wouldn't give them the satisfaction of a 'sir'. He slapped me across the side of my head making me stagger.

'I'll teach you respect, boy. I'll teach you respect if it's the last thing I do. You're the scum of the earth, some of you. But I'll teach you respect, you see if I don't. What do you think you're doing climbing in the window?'

My ear was stinging with a fierce heat like it does when you come into a warm room on a winter-frosted day. 'If I didn't climb in the window, I'd have to stand in the queue.'

'Well, what's wrong with standing in the queue? Everybody else stands in the queue.'

When the bell went you had to line up in fours. In silence. The prefects kept you parading there in order to relish their little ration of power. They were learning to be pigs, grasses, grunts, petty officials. Their smart school uniforms made it a dress rehearsal for the parts they were to play in later life. Bigger kids would tread on your heels or trip you, shove you into the kid in front or shoulder you out of the queue where you were pounced on, as vulnerable as small rodents to birds of prey. Prefects were allowed the privilege of administering punishment.

The teacher's whine broke off. The glazed expression in my

69

eyes must have told him he was talking to himself. He cracked his hand hard across the side of my face again. I fell against a desk. I could feel the heat spreading across my face like a stain. I saw his expression change to one of satisfaction as tears formed in my eyes. I held on to them. 'You're not even listening, boy. Look at me when I speak to you. Look at me!'

I looked at the blurred polished wooden bricks of the floor, set at angles to each other, as though petrified in permanent conflict.

'I've had a bellyful of your insolence, boy. Get to the head-master's room. Some of you will never learn. You're a total waste of my time and effort. You don't deserve the advantages you have, nor the money that's spent on you.' I moved towards the door but my slowness infuriated him so that he jabbed his fingers stiffly into my back. 'Come on, lad. Hurry it up!'

Apart from being jerked a couple of steps forward I continued at my own chosen speed. He pushed past me in exasperation and stormed out of the classroom.

The headmaster's office was just inside the main entrance that we kids were not allowed to use. At first there was plenty of bustle in the corridor. Smaller lads stared with fear or admiration. Bigger ones laughed or taunted. Later the corridor was deserted. I leaned against a radiator to warm my bum and the back of my legs. Opposite me was a painting: a cart with hay on, a pond, a little wooden boy. Further along another picture: an old sailor with a pipe, mending a net, another little boy – not wooden this one but spongy. It was no place for real little boys of flesh and blood.

A woman came out of the secretary's office. She passed without looking at me and knocked on the headmaster's door, bending her head to listen for his summons. She went inside. I waited, my chest a cavern of apprehension. The door opened and the secretary came out clutching a handful of letters. She peered at me with loathing through thick-lensed spectacles as if I was a crab she had found among her pubic hair. 'You may go in now,' she said.

Cunt, I said in my mind. I walked slowly into the big room trying not to let my fear show. The headmaster sat effetely behind the barrier of his huge desk like a captain of industry, like a high court judge, elbows placed carefully on the padded leather arms of his chair, velvet fingertips delicately touching.

He stared at me without speaking for a while. He pulled out a lacy hanky from his sleeve, wiped it back and forth across the tip of his large nose and tucked it back into his sleeve again. His voice was cultured, and as soft as engine oil. 'I'm sorry to see you here again so soon.'

There was no sorrow in his voice.

'I don't understand you. I don't understand you at all. We provide you with every opportunity to improve yourself, better yourself ...'

I closed the shutters. It was dark inside and peaceful. He threw words at me like rotten fruit at someone held helplessly in the stocks, but I was safe inside a crystal coffin and the missiles splattered against the surface and slithered off. Gradually his words became stones that rebounded and fell among millions of other worthless and wasted words that made a rubbish tip out of his room.

I stared at the polished wood and inlaid leather of his desk top, as big as a double bed. A lively swirl of bright colour was imprisoned in a dead weight of heavy glass. A gold stiletto paperknife, like an assassin's weapon, lay beside the unmarked blotter. Black, red and green pens stood erect in an elaborate ebony inkwell set. Everything was slightly larger than life, like the belongings of a small giant. A heavy and gleaming brass ashtray lay on the side of the desk nearest to me. I fantasised picking it up with my two hands and smashing it down with all my strength on the man's head, and his look of surprise as the blood began flowing down his forehead and flooding into his eyes.

The headmaster got up and crossed the carpet silently to the long narrow corner cupboard. I looked out of the window, across the green playing field, where no one was playing, to the iron railings which cut the children off from the outside world. I stared through, and beyond, those prison bars. Regulation houses were ranged in even rows. Tall grey lamp standards stood like sentinels at regular intervals. I wondered whether they were a cleverly disguised surveillance system, prying into every moment of our private lives.

The swish of the cane slicing the air brought me back sharply into the room. The headmaster examined the cane critically like a dealer considering a purchase. He turned away, his black gown swinging behind him – a medieval inquisitor. He re-

71

placed the cane and selected another. Bent it between his hands. Slashed it twice through the air, watching me, to assess the effect of his little drama.

'It's no good talking to you, is it? You never listen.' *It's no good talking to you*, I thought. *You never listen*. 'There's only one thing you boys understand.'

He sliced the air with the cane again and oozed slowly towards me. His eyes widened. His mouth was pulled back, revealing regular little teeth, in a grimace of anticipation. He was tall. He seemed rigid. He moved stiffly. His nostrils quivered. His upper lip twitched. Tall and thin and pale, the black gown made him seem taller, thinner, paler. He motioned me towards a small table. I glanced at the window and fantasised dashing across the room, shattering through the glass, and making a break for freedom. I thought about Billy all those years before and wondered what he would do here, now. I walked to the table, bent forward across it, and felt for the far edge with my fingers. I gripped. Closed my eyes. Clenched my teeth. Held my breath. I felt the bony vampire pull my jacket up my back and slide his pale hands gently around both cheeks of my arse. Then nothing. Then the pain.

After leaving the welfare office I wandered around the streets in the cold air till I felt calmer. I came across a newsagent's and discovered, to my delight, it was the day the local weekly newspaper was published. There were several places to let. One was a furnished house going very cheap. I ran all the way, stopping breathlessly only to ask for directions.

The house to be let was not the address advertised. A young woman answered the door and took me round to a nearby street. It was a small stone terraced house in a dirty cul-de-sac. It had two dingy downstairs rooms, a back kitchen and two bedrooms. The landlady wore a short, imitation-fur jacket and tight trousers. I could see the outline of her scanty pants and she swung her backside for me as I followed her from room to room and up the stairs. Only fear of losing the house prevented me from grabbing hold of her in the bedroom. The sparse furnishing looked as if it had been bought in junk shops. Bits and pieces old ladies who passed their last years in poverty left behind when they died. The things their relations didn't want.

I told her I hadn't brought much money out with me and left her all I'd got for a deposit. I knew Bud would lend me enough for a month's rent. I got a list of second-hand shops from her and spent the rest of the day searching for baby things: cot, bath, pram, and so on. I ordered a number of items and had them put by for me.

Having no money, and no luck in getting a lift, I had to walk back to the site. It was dark by the time I arrived. I was tired, but happy. I felt like a primitive man coming home after a successful hunt. Bud and Anne weren't in. Sheila was sitting on the side of their bed. 'Hello, love,' I said. 'How are you feeling?'

'Where have you been?' Her voice was so cold it burned. It was as shocking as having a bucket of dirty water slung in my face.

My mother was always sickly. She suffered with anaemia. Whenever she had a period she became bitter, short-tempered and violent. Bursting like shrapnel. Set off like a booby trap by the least wrong move. I knew her periods, though I didn't know what caused them, because when she hoisted her skirt to warm herself in front of that little bedroom grate, she smelled. She smelled like brussels sprouts going bad. When she smelled she was worst. I grew to hate and fear her smell.

Her blood group was B rhesus negative. Though she was anaemic she was on call from the city hospital. If they needed blood of her blood group they would send for her, since there was none in their bank. Men would come pounding frighteningly on our door, like Nazis coming for Jews or socialists, startling us out of our nightmares late at night or in the early hours of the morning. A pub fight, perhaps, or a back-street abortion gone wrong, or a road accident. I would be left alone with my fears while she was taken away in the ambulance, the blue light flashing its urgency and the bell frantically signalling a warning at the corner at the bottom of the street.

I used to picture the victim, the dark grey of the hospital blanket accentuating the deathly whiteness of his face. With all his living colour drained away and the imperceptible shallowness of his breathing he might have been already dead. Then she would be wheeled in to lie passively beside him, and the tube connected to the needle in her artery, her blood pumping into him, her small stream of life (as she herself was drained) bringing the man back from the dead. And when no longer needed, she was dumped, pale and corpse-like, back on our doorstep.

Then she would sit, in the night, on the oval tin box that was her fireside seat, her feet in the grate of the small bedroom fireplace in our living room, trying to soak up the fire's weak

74

warmth into her deathly cold body. I would get up to try to take care of her. I'd hover anxiously behind her like a mother watching over a sick child. I'd make tea. Once I fell at the turn of the unlit staircase carrying the kettle from the kitchen and scalded my chest and arms with water just off the boil. She didn't have the strength to help me. Sometimes she fainted. Once she fell into the fire. I dragged her clear, hardly able to move the heavy, dead weight. I beat out the smoke from the smouldering, blackened area of cardigan on her shoulder. She lay awkwardly twisted across the rag rug, spilling over the fender into the grate.

Men came and went from the room. From our lives. They passed through her, gratifying themselves. Forcing their way between her tight defences. Withdrawing to lick their wounds, leaving her dissatisfied, angry, loathing them, and her own body. And hating me. Hating my sex. I was the rotten fruit of a blighted tree, growing daily more like that lonely boy she had loved. And hated.

One evening she was getting ready for a date. She'd tried hard, with little money, to make herself look desirable, modelling herself on Hollywood's image of the *femme fatale*. Woolworth make-up. Club twin-set. Home perm. I stood behind her brushing her hair. She sat on the edge of the tin box, waiting. Expectantly, waiting. Glancing continually at the green alarm clock on the mantelpiece, while I went on brushing. Me brushing. She waiting. Half past seven turned to eight o'clock. And then half past eight. The man didn't come. My hate for her evaporated with the passing time. Brushing and waiting. She so pale. So old-young. Frail-strong. Hunched on the little box. Her imitation pearls too dull even to catch the light thrown out by the gas mantle on the wall. Waiting for a lover who never came. And me feeling such pity and sympathy because I knew, and knew she knew by then, he was not going to come. She seemed to diminish on the box as the time passed, and I reached out a tender hand and gently patted the small fragile victim on the head, searching among a flood of feeling to salvage some words of kindness.

'There, there. You poor little skunk.'

Her body jerked as though she was under ECT. 'What? What did you call me?'

75

I stepped back a pace, surprised and scared. 'I ... I only meant ...'

'What did you call me?' She stood up and took the hairbrush out of my hand. She was like a steel spring coiled tight under pressure.

'A skunk,' I whispered.

When you read this, put down the book. Go to your kitchen and fetch a wooden spoon, or fetch a coathanger or hairbrush from the bedroom, or anything similar that comes to hand. Stand by your bed, or an armchair. Try to beat the stuffing out of it.

I didn't ask for it. They just grabbed me, and dragged me out. Out of the warm, comforting dark, into the harsh, white, artificial light. And then they bashed me, slashed me, and when I screamed I got smashed for screaming. They screwed me up and threw me down and knocked me to hell and back, so now I'm black and blue, bruised and wounded. And they look at my scars and tell me I'm ugly.

And they're right.

I went to Sheila and bent to kiss her mouth but she turned her face away. I felt anger collecting like sediment in my stomach, but I held on to it and kissed her cheek gently. I sat beside her and put my arm round her shoulders. 'Listen, I've got a house for us.' She turned her head sharply to look at me. I tried to smile but the skin of my face was tight and wouldn't let me. 'I've found a house,' I said. 'A whole house all to ourselves'.

'How can we afford it?'

'Don't worry about that. We've got a house. That's the main thing. You've got a place where your baby can be born.'

'What house?'

'It's great. It's a little terrace house in the town. Two bedrooms, back yard, kitchen, everything.' I tried to penetrate the thickness of her ice with the warmth of my enthusiasm. I expected that as the reality of what I was saying dawned on her, she would throw her arms round me and kiss me. But she sat staring at me as if I'd told her the baby inside her had died. 'Everything's going to be all right, Sheila.'

'Don't you think I'd like to choose where I'm going to live for myself?'

'Well, sure. But we didn't have much choice, did we? I mean, I've found a house.'

'And it didn't occur to you to consult me about it?'

'I thought you'd be pleased.'

'You've got no idea, have you?'

Her contempt was like ether on my skin which was numbed, and like paraffin on my anger which flared up, lifting me onto my feet. 'What are you on about? Look, for Chrissake, I've been walking around all day till my legs are nearly worn down to my fucking knees trying to sort things out – trying to make things all right – for *you*.'

'Don't raise your voice to me.'

She spoke cold hard words like pieces of jagged steel from factory waste. Like a teacher who despises children. Like a mother who detests her child. My hands formed themselves into fists. 'Raise my fucking voice? What's my fucking voice got to do with it? I've found you a fucking house, you bleeding ungrateful selfish fucking cunt!'

She heaved herself up and walked away from me towards the door. 'Don't speak to me until you can speak decently.'

'Don't fucking walk away from me, you cunt!' I followed her and, grabbing her arm, twisted her towards me.

She looked me icily and contemptuously in the face. She spoke in a quiet, calm, authoritative voice. 'Take your hands off me.'

I punched her on the side of the head. She fell against the sink and went down on one knee. Then struggled up and went out of the door closing it quietly behind her. I stood staring at the door for a long time, unable to move. Then I sat heavily on the bed with my head in my hands.

After a while I dried my face with a teacloth. I went to the door and stared out into the blackness. I called her name several times. Once my eyes had got used to the dark I went out and stumbled around the muddy churned-up site looking for her. I got cold and went back into the caravan. I put the kettle on and made a pot of tea. Sheila came in shivering, with mud halfway up her calves. We stood eyeing each other warily. 'I'm sorry, love,' I said. 'I'm really sorry.'

I made a move towards her so I could cuddle her but she stepped back. She had a hunted animal expression on her face. I looked down at the floor. I couldn't bear to look at her. 'Come and get warm,' I said, 'and have a cup of tea.' I poured two cups. Then I looked in the food cupboard. She edged past without touching me and went to sit on the bed. I found some bread and marge and jam. After we'd eaten I washed up.

We were still making love when Bud and Anne came back.

It was at the time we moved into this house that I began to have a recurring dream. It isn't always exactly the same – but the variations are small.

It is night. I am with another man. We are going to fetch my motor. Through a small side door we enter a huge, cold hangar of a garage housing dozens of cars. It is dark. I can't even see my own feet. I have to move slowly for fear of bumping into something. I thread my way through the maze of vehicles until I come to mine. I look for my key. My friend has gone to open the cumbersome main concertina doors.

Out of the darkness, from behind the vehicles, as if emerging from under the ground, come three nude women armed with knives. They slice and slash and chop and stab. I try to defend myself, but I am cut again and again. My blood spurts from me, like water from a multi-punctured hose, spraying and decorating the bare bodies of my female butchers.

I see my friend over by the partly opened door in the spotlight of a street lamp. He is me. A naked assassin is hacking at him. He slides slowly down the door. His fingers, unable to find a grip on the cold smooth corrugated iron, paint a wavering tracery like the zig-zag pattern of a tyre tread. Her breasts are bathed in his blood.

The three women renew their flashing steel assault on this other me as I watch my dying. My life blood steams in the lamp light, and streams from me, and I feel my strength draining.

I picked up my first girlfriend on the sea front on an autumn evening. I walked her home balancing my bike with one hand and holding onto her hand with the other. It felt as though she was leading me out of hell. We stood against the side wall of her house and kissed. My legs trembled so much I had to lean on her or I would have fallen down. I was clumsy, anxious to learn. She pressed my hand on her breast. A current passed through the circuit of our bodies. I came in my jeans. Then she invited me in for a cup of tea.

The house was affluently messy. She left me in the kitchen and disappeared into the bowels of the house. I felt trapped. There was a dark stain, like an ink blot, by my groin. I tried to hide it with my hands. A girl who I guessed was her sister glided through the kitchen, ignoring me, and went out of the back door. Then the mother came. She asked me where Claire had gone. I opened my mouth, but then I realised I didn't know which of the girls she was referring to. The girl I'd been touching hadn't told me her name. I stood with my hands clasped in front of my genitals, my jaw slack, feeling like an ape escaped from a zoo. The sister saved me by re-entering the kitchen, and her mother said, 'Oh, there you are.'

'Yes,' I said. 'Here she is.' The mother gave me a funny look.

We had tea in the sitting room around a television set. Claire sat on the arm of her father's chair. I found myself staring at them. She had an arm around his shoulders in apparent affection. The mother asked me what I thought of their new wallpaper. It was on the wall opposite the bay window. A pattern of vines over trellis. The other walls were painted white. I scrabbled through my head in panic for something to say while she babbled on. 'Don't you think it makes the room look bigger? Seems to push that wall back.'

'Yeah. Trouble is you won't have so much space in the other room,' I said.

The woman laughed disproportionately. Her chortling made me think of the cackling of the old crones at work.

The first job I got when I left school was in a plastics factory. The noise hammered at my mind and drilled into my eardrums. Men worked the big presses wearing a permanent pained frown, their eyes almost closed as if trying to shut out the noise from their heads. They communicated with signs and gestures. I trundled a basket up and down the metal aisles. The men would sometimes look at me and wink or smile, or shout some comment I couldn't hear.

I collected finished work and transported it to the sorting room where the rubber doors flapping behind me held the noise at bay. It was like coming to an oasis after a trek across a desert. But it was an oasis with a plague of flies in the shape of old and ugly women who never tired of tormenting me. The young girls laughed at the women's crudities, or ignored me altogether.

'I bet you're big for your age, duckie. Let's have a look.' The women screeched as though wanting the world to hear, above the chatter and clatter and piped music, that they weren't beaten down. There was still life in the old girls yet.

''Ere y'are, Mary. He'll be just the right size for you.'

'Gerrout. He's still got the cradle marks on his bum.'

'That's all right, gel. You wanna catch 'em young, then you can train 'em proper.'

'I'm not that hard up, ta.'

'I bet he's hard up, though. Let's have a feel then, luvvy.'

The shrieks of the women would merge with the shrieking of the machines as I retreated unhappily through the rubber doors and trundled my skip along the gangways, isolated in a cocoon of noise.

It's funny to think back and to realise that if one small thing had been different the whole direction of your life would have been changed. We're like runaway trains passing over points on every metre of track. Every day contains a hundred possibilities. And yet at the end of the line it all seems so inevitable that we should have arrived wherever we are.

If I hadn't met that girl ... If she hadn't given me that kiss ... If it hadn't been raining so heavily ... If someone unknown hadn't left their car ...

I asked her her name before I left. She told me it was Annette. She kissed me goodbye with astonishing passion in the kitchen and I was sent out into a dark downpour feeling deliriously happy. My bicycle saddle was wet. I rode with my arse in the air pretending to be racing in the Tour de France. The rain was driving into my face. On the main road I ran into the back of a black car parked without lights. I rolled along the roof, bounced onto the bonnet, and plunged painfully into a puddle on the road. My front wheel was buckled and the bicycle frame broken. It was a long walk home.

I crept quietly into the dark kitchen. I took off my sodden jacket, hung it on the back of a chair, and rubbed my hair with a teacloth. My mother came into the room and switched on the light. I put the teacloth down quickly onto the draining board. She'd been sleeping by the fire. She was still dressed but her stockings were rolled down round her ankles. Her legs were blotchy – mauve and red and white, her ankles swollen. Her cardigan was ruckled up and the zip of her skirt undone showing part of her grubby pink slip. Her eyes were puffy and half closed and she made a bad mouth.

'Where have you been till this time?'

'I had an accident on my bike.'

85

'I should think so – riding about at this time of night. Where have you been?'

'Somebody's house.'

'Whose house?'

'What difference does it make whose house?'

'Don't you cheek me. I'll thrash you, big as you are.' I'd heard it all before. So often. I sighed. 'And don't sigh at me. And wipe that grin off your face too, or I'll make you smile on the other side of your face, my lad.'

I hadn't realised I was smiling. I tried to make my face straight, but not knowing what expression I was getting rid of, my face became ridiculous. She slapped me. 'Don't you be rude to me. Now, where have you been?' I said nothing. 'Where have you been?' I looked inward and ran a film of what was to come on a screen at the back of my brain. I saw a frenzied fool fighting a duel with an empty suit of armour. 'Give me that!' I reached the serving spoon from the draining board and handed it to her.

'How many times have I told you to be in this house by half past ten?'

'And how many times have I told you ...'

The first crack burned like a brand.

'Remember who you're speaking to.'

'Look – if I go to ...'

The second caught me in exactly the same place as the first. I heard on the radio once that they could identify which were the slaves among remains from ancient times found in Egypt by the fractured forearm, caused presumably by the warding off of blows.

'Don't you "look" me.'

I took a deep breath. 'The pictures don't finish till twenty past ten, so I can't get a bus before half past, so how can I get home before eleven?'

'Well, what have you got a bike for?'

'I haven't any more, and anyway if I cycle I still can't get home after the film before eleven, can I?'

'I've told you before till I'm blue in the face – you'll just have to leave before the end.'

'Why should I?'

'Because I'm your mother, that's why. And I didn't slog and

86

slave and work my fingers to the bone for you all these years so that you could speak to me just as you like.'

'God, I wish I'd never been bloody well born.'

'You what?' She started thrashing about wildly like a demented dervish. 'Don't you dare talk to me like that. I'm not having you swearing at me. I'm your mother and don't you forget it.' The spoon cracked across my skull and span away through the air. She started slapping me then, till her hands hurt, and then grabbed up a fish slice from the frying pan on the gas stove. She was pulling me around the room with one hand and hitting out with the fish slice with the other so that gobs of cold grease splattered onto my face and hair and jumper. She babbled hysterically, long-nursed grievances bursting out of her like shrapnel from a bomb, harboured pain flooding through her bruised child's body, contaminating the next in line. 'I'm your mother and you can't do a thing I ask. I work morning and night to try to keep body and soul together, to try to keep a roof over your head, and you can't even do as you're told. You *will* come home of an evening. Do you hear me? You *will* come home at a decent hour. I'm not having you defy me – big as you are. I'm not having it. You'll do as you're told or you'll answer to me.'

When she was too tired to go on, I looked with scorn into her eyes and there I read that she too had realised. The black magic she had worked on me for ten years was based on my fear, but now the spell was broken. A witch stripped of her power is at the mercy of the claws of the cat. She was impotent – and I was no longer a child.

I went to bed aching from the accident and the beating. Instinct warned me that the deposed are dangerous. I was concerned lest she stab me in my sleep. I saw it like a film in my mind's eye. The crazed woman continuously plunging a carving knife into the raw red meat of my unguarded body, the metal tongue opening bleeding mouths of mutilation, the steel blade raping wounds-like-vaginas gushing vermilion fountains, my blood sloshing on the bed covers, spraying the walls, splattering the ceiling, and staining her hands and arms and face.

Tiredness dragged at me like quicksand. I struggled to stay awake so that I could defend myself. She hadn't gone to bed.

I could hear her in the next room crying with frustration and hatred and self-pity. I thought about Annette, and the feel of her breasts beneath the soft wool of her jumper and I felt myself hard and strong. I masturbated and fell asleep. Next day I left home and found a room of my own.

When I got sacked from my first job I took the first holiday I'd ever had. I stayed in a bed and breakfast place for a week in autumn. With my bedroom window open I could hear the gulls crying my pain out over the sea.

I spent long grey days watching new-born waves hurl themselves at ancient rocks only to be flung back in disintegrating confusion. Occasionally I swam, despite the rain, although the loneliness and the sea wind were cold. Day after day I wandered miles along the deserted shore haunted by ghosts of childhood, searching for a girl who might throw me a life-line and drag me into manhood.

On the last night of my stay I did meet someone. Pam was fourteen, but very experienced. She boasted to me that she'd gone on a school boat trip and while the teacher sat with the pupils on deck she'd gone below and been screwed in turn by every member of the crew. Her boyfriend was twenty-three. That night he'd gone out with another girl. I think she did what she did with me to spite him.

She led me by the hand along the cliff path to a wooden hut. There, sheltered from the drizzle and cold wind, she lay on her back on the narrow bench and I lay on top of her. I kissed her but her face was cold and damp, and her jumper was unpleasantly wet when I groped for her breasts. She became impatient and turned her face away while she fumbled with my fly. I felt her freezing fingers on my cock, but couldn't be sure that she'd put it inside her. I experienced a warm tingling sensation as we moved against each other. I looked out of the open side of the hut, straining my ears for the sound of footsteps. I could see a necklace of lights around the throat of the night where a line of fishing boats was anchored on the horizon. I wondered if I was really doing it, and if this was all it was.

I had fled from school when I was fifteen and from home when I was sixteen. I went from one job to another: factories; warehouses; shops; building sites. I quickly grew sick of the work, and the foremen quickly grew sick of me. I hated and resented those boring and useless hours being gouged out of my life. I pushed barrowloads of wet cement till my hands blistered and the blisters burst and bled, staining the barrow handles brown. I screwed tiny screws that secured speakers into transistor radios until my wrists ached like an ancient arthritic's. I immersed myself in the gore and guts of the slaughter-house where the carcases steamed in the cold air and the blood and shit stank and the animals screamed a fear that was my own. I washed second-hand cars, touching up over the rust, and painting old tyres black to look like new. I filled tanks with petrol and sumps with oil, hating the smell of work on my clothes and skin. I scraped shuttering boards in the bitter wind and biting rain, pulling old nails like teeth. I shovelled gravel and sand, stacked bricks that tore at my hands like brambles, humped lorryloads of pipes and rods and bags of cement – heavy, mindless work that I could enjoy for a few hours in the sunshine but which turned into endless torment when my back ached or my hands were cut or the cold hammered nails into my body while time slowed down like an old man with scarcely strength enough to put one foot in front of the other.

Life only began when work ended, and the purpose of life was to fuck girls. I flitted like a bee among artificial flowers from one to another finding nothing to sustain me. My first steady was still at school. Her mother, a fat cockney who kept a pot of tea stewing over a small light from the time she got up till the time she went back to bed, courted boys for her pretty daughter.

Laura was passive, like putty in my hands. The first time I got her alone I fucked her brutally, kneading her tits like dough. I thrust into her, feeling hard and powerful, watching pain, like a dark bird, in her face. Tears dribbled across her cheeks and chin and pain made her ugly. But once the strength had drained out of me I saw a child's face, hurt and unhappy. I stroked hair from her cheeks and forehead where strands stuck in the tears and sweat, and kissed her gently.

My life took on an unchanging shape as though I had allowed a mould to be lowered over it. I went to Laura's for food and a fuck, Sunday, Monday, Tuesday, and Thursday. Wednesday, Friday, and Saturday, I went out with my mate, Bud, hunting for hole. I became a compulsive gambler playing for sex along the sea front. My winnings were as satisfying as candy floss to a starving man.

I felt trapped: trapped in the shoebox of a room I lived in on my own; trapped by the cancer of dull and depressing work; trapped by Laura's moronic desire to settle down in a nice little mortgaged semi and gloat over babies her mother fondly imagined would sweep the board at beautiful baby competitions around the country. Laura's little claws were hooked deep into my flesh, and worse, her gross mother was sitting on me so heavily I was suffocating.

It was summer and I was working as an ice-cream salesman driving my van around estates where the harassed mothers least able to afford it were hassled into buying overpriced lollies for undernourished children. By the time I'd cashed in, cleaned up, and got to Laura's it was late and her old ones were established in front of the television for the evening in the lounge. I ate a warmed-up dinner in the kitchen.

In the back room I sat watching Laura selecting records. She felt carefully for the erect knob of the record player and eased the pile of records gently down over it. She was a beautiful girl in a bland sort of way. She wasn't yet plump but the suggestion was there that she would spread like her mother in middle age. She'd been squashed into submissiveness by her mother – made into easy prey for a domineering man. She did as told in a joyless way that would bring joy to no one. I told her to come and she came. I told her to sit on my lap and she sat. The needle scratched onto the first record. *Dream lover, where are you – with a love, oh so true*? I kissed her and ran my hands over her breasts and thighs as automatically as turning on the ignition and pulling out the choke before starting a car. I felt a tenderness for her, but it was a hostage, walled up inside me, blocked off from words or actions. I told her to take her pants off and she did so. I screwed them small and stuffed them into my pocket. She looked at me mournfully. 'Paul, can I suck you tonight?' she whined. 'Please. It's the dangerous time.'

I watched her perform and my pride swelled like a tumour. I held her hair in my fist, like a butcher hauling a sheep to the slaughter, working her head up and down slow and steady to the rhythm of *Don't be cruel, to a heart that's true*, until I groaned the tension out of my body into her mouth.

There would be tears, hysterics and threats of suicide later in the evening but at that moment Laura was still dreaming of the diamond ring her mother kept offering to lend me the money to buy. But that afternoon in my ice-cream van, fooling myself with the thought that I was opting for 'freedom', I'd decided that this would be my last visit. This knowledge aroused in me a sense of power over Laura and inflated my feeling of virility. I ordered her to sit on me. She reluctantly steered my sex gingerly into hers and arranged her pleated skirt modestly to make a secret of our union. 'You will be careful, Paul, won't you?' she whimpered. The record player made a few clicks and then hummed quietly while she writhed on me like a living insect stuck on an entomologist's pin. Till the door danced open. Laura's mother waddled in, labouring for breath as if she'd just run with the torch from Mount Olympus, bearing a tray of drinking chocolate and biscuits. She pulled up a chair and slumped onto it like a four-hundredweight sack of potatoes.

'Ooh, you missed a luverly filum,' she said, and went on to recount the story from beginning to end. I lost track about half-way through but tried my best to maintain a look of pleasant interest on my face. Laura sat demurely with her cup of drinking chocolate in her hand looking as though she was at a vicarage tea party. My hardness was stuck up into the soft wet warmth of her like a knife in an undercooked sponge cake. My consciousness became centred on a feeling of hot throbbing pleasure as a flame burned its way along the fuse towards the stick of gelignite. When the explosion came Laura tensed, squeezing everything out of me, and her cup and spoon rattled on the saucer. I laid my head back, feeling as lively as a wrung-out dish rag, and closed my eyes. The woman hammered her harsh voice into my brain like the nail of a headache. 'What's a matter with *you*, Paul?'

'Eh?'

'What's a matter with you?'

'Oh, nothing. Just a bit tired, that's all.'

She flushed, angry that I hadn't been paying attention, her eyes bulging like a rabbit with myxomatosis. 'You'd better get off home to bed then. You two have far too many late nights. I'm always telling you but I might as well talk myself blue in the face for all the notice you take of me. Come on then, Laura, get up off him so he can get hisself home.'

Laura turned into a pillar of salt. My pillar of flesh stood firm. I tried to steady my voice. 'Let's just finish our drinks, Mum. Then I'll be off.'

Six weeks later, on a Saturday, Laura turned up at my room. 'Paul, I need to talk to you,' she said.

'Get undressed,' I said.

Afterwards, I was lying smugly by her side with my eyes closed, like a cat that's polished off the cream. She said, 'I'm preggers.'

Without moving I opened one eye and peered at the profile of her pretty face. Her cow-brown eyes stared at the ceiling in a theatrical way as if she was a third-rate actress playing Joan of Arc hearing voices. 'You what?' I said.

'I'm preggers.'

The word made me fume. Why couldn't she say she was up the fucking spout or something? I stared at her for a while without speaking. She was not yet sixteen. She looked older. Old enough to be my mother. I despised her. 'Whose is it?' I asked spitefully.

She sighed. 'Whose do you think?'

'I wouldn't know.'

'Well, it's yours.'

As if I didn't know. I'd been the only one. I felt as though I was drowning. A sudden urge swept over me to cradle her, to take care of her, to convince her that we could live happily ever after. Then a wave of distrust. I wondered if she was deceiving me, making a fool of me. Perhaps she feared she'd got pregnant by some other fucker after I'd left, or maybe she was using me to help her get away from the grizzly-bear-like embrace of her mother. The next wave was hatred: hatred for her satin skin, her body soft as a ripe fruit, soon to be over-ripe, growing more and more gross until it became as grotesque as her mother's (fucking her would be like fucking a dumpling or jerking off into a jelly); hatred for her perfectly proportioned and stupid face, round as a full moon, blank as a balloon. It suddenly struck me that the strange thing about her face was its symmetry. It was empty – there was no character in it. I wondered if she was hollow, the runaway sex object of some lunatic scientist, the world's first rubber lady, and whether it was possible to learn to live with someone you didn't love. The next flood of feeling was for the baby. I felt it would be a crime to abandon it to the mercy of her inadequacy; and decided that no bugger was going to do to a baby of mine what those bastards had done to me. At seventeen, it seemed, I had already forged the steel for my own shackles.

The next nine months were a nightmare. Three times we were evicted when the landladies discovered Laura was pregnant. Days I spent either in the drudgery of dull employment, or seeking it. I passed the evenings pounding pavements looking at a succession of depressing rooms in dirty houses where springs reached out of armchair seats like the arms of drowning men from the sea and mattresses stank of piss. We ended up in an attic room, with no windows except for a skylight in the roof, and a little cooker on the landing, on condition that we left before the baby was born. The rent took two thirds of my wage. There was not enough left over to eat properly. Laura sank into a depression in which she imagined all sorts of demons of ill-health were destroying her and either stayed in bed or sat hunched over the single-bar electric fire.

Being in that one-eyed room was like having fallen down a manhole. The only glimmer of hope was a tiny patch of sky beyond our reach. And yet Laura hardly ever left that pit. She seemed incapable of coping with even the smallest tasks and I found myself taking care of the shopping and cooking and cleaning as well as earning the bread. Finally, when she was eight months, I took her out to the most expensive restaurant in the town. We had the best. Then I called the manager and told him I couldn't pay the bill. I was kept in prison till Bud bailed me out. Later I was found guilty of obtaining credit by fraud and given a fine I never paid. And after nine months of sordid apprehension when I finally felt some excitement about the magic of birth, the carefully counted days dragged themselves through unbelievable weeks of waiting. It seemed our baby, Josephine, had sense enough to be unwilling to venture from womb-warmth out into the unwelcoming world.

96

Laura proved incapable of taking care of her baby. When I went to work in the morning I left Laura a list of jobs to do and shouted at her in the evening when I discovered they hadn't been done. Often I would come home carrying the weariness of work to find the baby still in her cot, crying. Yellow shit would be oozing from plastic pants, the sheet by her face creamy-wet with puke.

On the days Laura got up and went out she became plasticine in the hands of men she met in the street, men who were startled at her prettiness, surprised by her compliance. When I found Laura in our bed with a man he pulled the sheet over his head as though his inability to see me made him invisible. I sat in the other room nursing a blade-wound of bleeding pride till I heard him leave.

But usually Laura would be in bed alone, sleeping, or gazing at the ceiling which was the screen for her dreams, or writing letters she never sent.

Dear David,

I simply have to write to you to tell you how I feel. I am so full today. My cup brimmeth over. I am lying in bed listening to some heart-stirring music on the radio. I adore Mahler, don't you? The sun is shining into the bedroom. I can hear birds singing. Dear little Josephine is sleeping like an angel by my side.

Mahler? Laura didn't know the difference between Mahler and Mantovani!

97

'Laura, for fuck's sake! Look at this child again. What's the matter with you?' She stared sulkily from where she sat propped up by pillows in the bed. 'Oh, what's the fucking use! Have you given this kid anything to eat today?'

'She had her bottle.'

'Hasn't she had any proper food? Didn't you buy any? I told you to this morning. I bloody wrote it down for you.' She sat as sullen as a child. 'Bloody answer me when I speak to you. Have you bought any baby food?'

'I haven't been out yet.'

'Yet! It's gone bloody five o'clock. What do you do all day?'

'I don't know.'

'How can you just lie there all day doing nothing? You're like a dollop of lard melting in a fucking frying pan. You're just a bleeding great pile of refuse. What's the matter with you?'

I let Jo cry while I dragged off her mucky dress and nappy. Uncomfortable with guilt I cleaned her before I cuddled her. Once she was comforted I smeared cream over the angry nappy rash, dressed her, and carried her out into the fresh air. I left her clothes tumbling in the launderette while I bought a stock of baby food. Back home I fed her cold mush straight from the tin, and later I sang her to sleep and laid her on a dry towel in her cot.

Laura was making up in front of the mirror ready for going out.

'Laura?'

'Mm?'

'I can't go to work and look after Jo properly. She's eight months old. She should be heavier than she is. She should be crawling around. You don't take care of her. I want to get her adopted.'

She put on a floppy orange hat with a wide brim and looked at herself in the mirror, turning her head first one way, then the other. She looked stunning.

'Did you hear what I said?'

'Mm.' She bent the hat brim so that it curled down to one side.

'Well, do you agree?'

Ed, the mechanic, who lived downstairs, must have been having a row with his wife. Their two voices became locked into each other and came spiralling, piercingly, up from the flat below. There was a crash and the screaming stopped.

'Laura?'

'Yes, all right.'

'All right what?'

'Yes, I agree.'

'You agree to have her adopted?'

'Yes.'

'You'll sign the papers and everything?'

'Yes.'

I think I'd really been saying, I want you to look after the baby better. I hadn't thought she would agree. Suddenly I found myself staring into the frightening face of the reality of my words. I looked at her looking at herself. She appeared no more concerned than if I'd suggested leaving Jo with a baby-sitter for the evening.

'All right', I said quietly. 'I'll go to the office tomorrow.'

After she'd gone I sat for a long time on the edge of the bed, gazing at the sleeping baby in her cot. In every way it seemed better for her to be adopted. But I'd grown accustomed to her and feared losing her. It also meant that there would be no reason for me to stay with Laura, and even though it would be an understatement to say our marriage was a miserable failure, I dreaded being alone.

For several weeks I'd been on strike at home, refusing to clean up the flat, trying to force Laura to do it. Recognising our battles were now obsolete I set to work. There were used sanitary towels hidden in the breadbin. Dirty nappies in the oven. Old meat, a move with maggots, under a pile of unwashed clothing in the wardrobe. The mats were stuck to the floor with food. The cushions were stuck to the chairs. I found three baby's bottles brilliant with yellow milk and blue-green mould. White insects, like living crumbs, infested the furniture. Our home was like a witch's kitchen.

The day before Sophie was born Sheila and I were standing in the baby's bedroom with our arms around each other. Sheila looked happy. We kissed, her body hard against mine, the child coming between us. I eased her down onto the floor. Her hair, thick and rich, spilled across the cold lino. I supported my weight and kissed her long, ravishing her mouth with my tongue. I tugged her dress up to her stretched belly and ripped her pants off. 'I wish you wouldn't do that,' she said. 'I've no pants left.' I fumbled my hard cock out of my clothes and into her. She opened her mouth and closed her eyes. Taking my weight on both hands I lowered and raised myself slowly going deep into her and out again. Slowly in and out.

'Did you hear the one about the American with the bad heart?' I said.

'What are you talking about now?'

'There was this American,' I said, all the while fucking her gentle and slow and deep, 'and he went to the doctor. And he said, "Doctor, I get palpitations. My heart flutters like a dying bird." The doctor said, "Have a break. Take yourself on vacation to Mexico. And whenever you feel the palpitations, get down, wherever you are – if you're driving, get out of the car and get down at the side of the road – and do press-ups. Do press-ups till you feel better."'

I kissed her forehead, eyes, nose, cheeks, ears, lips, chin, neck, and she moaned like a cat purring.

'So he went to Mexico,' I said, 'and he was driving round, and he felt his palpitations start, his heart fluttering like a dying bird. So he got out of the car, and got down beside the road, and began to do press-ups. Like this.'

I began to move my whole body instead of just my pelvis. Each time I came down I kissed her, entered her with my cock and my tongue and came away again. 'And then . . .' Each time

101

I raised myself I opened my eyes and went on with the story. '... along came ...' Closed my eyes as I sank in. '... this Mexican ...' She lay with closed eyes, open to me. '... and he ...' Softly sinking into the soft wet warmth of her mouth and cunt and away out again. '... tapped him ...' Slowly in and out. '... on the shoulder ...' And I could feel the tension draining through my body and gathering throbbing in my cock. '... and said ...' I kept my eyes closed now and she gave a low quiet cow-like moan. '"... Señor ..."' Each time I sank in she moaned. '"... Señor ..."' Each time I sank in I wanted to stay, but forced myself up again and away. '"... the señorita ..."' And I plunged into her and her cunt seemed to clutch me, hold me, suck me, and she sucked my tongue into her mouth but I tore away, my voice thick like a drunk's. '"... the señorita – she gone now."' And as I went in she let out a slow mounting cry and mine became indistinguishable from hers and her body dragged the juice out of me spurting fast and then pumping slower and our bodies shuddered like two motors with each pulsing ejaculation.

And when it stopped I held myself there over her on trembling arms, resting lightly on her belly, with my head hanging and eyes closed, and then I keeled over slowly like a sinking ship and lay across her thighs at an angle from her, my arm thrown out, my hand holding gently onto her hair. 'When you're coming,' I mumbled, 'you want more plumbing. You wish your dong ... was a mile long.'

We lay there for several minutes silently. Then Sheila coughed and the contraction pushed me out. I got up lethargically and knelt beside her. She sat up and I saw that she'd been crying. 'What's a matter, china – wasn't that nice?'

'It's the best it's ever been.'

'Did you come?'

'Yes. It's the first time with you in me.'

'It'll get better and better.'

'Yes.'

'So why are you crying?'

'Oh, you know.'

'No.'

'The baby.'

'The baby? Everything's going to be all right.'

'I'm frightened.'

'There's no need to be frightened. Look at you. You're blooming with health. I never seen you look better since I met you. The baby's moving around, kicking, it's going to be all right.'

'I'm frightened of the hospital.'

'It'll be all right. I'll take care of you.'

'Will you?'

''Course I will.'

I held her face against my chest, massaged her back and kissed her head. By the time I'd helped her to her feet she'd begun to look happier again. I looked round the small dingy room, at the second-hand cot with its peeling Mickey Mouse transfer, and suddenly it was me who was crying.

'Paul?'

'I'm sorry.'

'What's the matter, darling?'

'I don't know. Its just . . . this place. It's a home. I never felt that about anywhere before.'

'Of course its a home, love. We'll make it a home.'

'Yeah. I know. Its just, being in this room and thinking of our kids. They can grow here – you know what I mean? This little room. They won't have to grow up like I did. They'll have a place of their own.'

Soon after being brought to this country, before memory, I was placed in a foster home. Then another. And then another. (I was a difficult child.) The first home was a farm. I remember a black and white border collie and a brown terrier; being set to ride on the broad and bony back of a cow; and the smoothness of snow pockmarked by a fox's footprints leading to the poultry run. Of the second home I remember only the path from the gate along the side of the house. At the third home there was a car that stood on bricks, covered like a cadaver with a tarpaulin sheet. It wasn't used and I was never allowed to play near it.

It is only in this last foster home that I remember the foster parents. They were a little old couple, wizened like crab apples. They were like story-book grandparents, although I don't think they had grandchildren, or even children, of their own. She always wore an apron over her dress, and her hands were red. He had glasses and a yellowish moustache and I think he was a retired watch repairer. But his hands, surprisingly, were big, and heavy like his wife's, and their tempers were short.

I think I must have lived there about a year, but I can only remember my mother coming to visit once. She brought a present of half a dozen toy soldiers. They had red coats and blue trousers and black busbies. They were bandsmen. One had a bass drum. One had a trombone. And so on. My mother came. I played with the soldiers. She came; then she started to leave. I didn't want her to go. The old couple clung onto me with spiteful hands while she went out to the hall and closed the door. I was crying. And struggling. Trying to break free from their grip, vicious as a vice. I heard the front door slam. I writhed away from their grasping hands and ran to the window. There was a bench round the inside of the bay. I climbed on it to look out.

She walked down the path. I beat on the window. I was

crying and calling out to her. She passed by the car without wheels that lay like a dead thing under its tarpaulin. She reached the gate and turned to wave gaily. She was smiling. I was screaming. Clawing at the glass. 'Mummy, Mummy, please don't go!' The old ones hovered behind me like hawks awaiting their moment. I scrabbled with my fingertips at that cold transparent incarcerating sheet of ice, like a frenzied gerbil scraping at the floor of its cage. I was crying, beside myself, crying and screaming. *Oh Mummy, don't go! Mummy, please don't go!*

She didn't look round again. After she'd walked a little way down the road, my guardians, like screws, grabbed me and dragged me away from the window. Dragged me with painful fingers like pincers into the middle of the room and started to smack me. Both of them shouting at me to shut up, furiously bashing and beating, frantically slapping and hitting, they hauled me upstairs and, like Broadmoor warders handling a murderous maniac, hustled me into the cupboard on the landing and locked the door.

There, in the darkness, I was left alone to learn by heart the lessons my life had to teach. Hope had been mutilated, love murdered, and trust trodden to dust under foot. Engraved on my mind I carry the memory of that birthday celebration, the day I was five years old.

My mother had been sent away by her mother when she was five years old. The oldest of four children. A consignment delivered to the steps of Doctor Barnardo's Home. Whoever called it a home must have been joking. It wasn't a home – it was a chamber of horrors. The place in Stepney was a reception and allocation centre. The girl sat on the steps in the draughty hall and the three little ones – one a baby in her arms – cried. A woman came by, a woman who, probably, had never been allowed to be a child herself. 'Can't you stop them making that noise!' she snapped.

They separated the children. First they'd been taken away from their mother. Then they were taken away from each other. In the end there were six children from that woman in Barnardo's homes. And they say you can't get blood from a stone.

My mother grew up in a northern town in a home run by three unmarried sisters. The maids were girls who'd grown up as inmates and all the inmates were girls. The eldest sister bullied the other two. The sisters bullied the maids. The maids bullied the girls. The bigger girls took it out on the younger ones. What else could you expect?

The girls lived in the back yard. The yard was confined by brick walls. Bricks made from clay that had been hauled from the earth's belly years before by children aged seven, eight, nine – children working fifteen-hour shifts and falling asleep almost the moment they climbed from the holes they worked in. The yard was surfaced with asphalt, thick and final and grey-black. Not even a blade of grass pierced it. There was a line painted across the yard. The girls had to toe the line like soldiers on a parade ground. They toed the line for everything. Even to clean their teeth.

A maid came down the line of girls with a jam jar full of water, and the girls dipped their toothbrushes in. They stood holding their brushes carefully angled so as not to spill the water globules clinging to the bristles. Then the maid came down the line with a tin of tooth powder, a mixture of camphor and chalk, like the stuff used in prisons, and the girls dipped their brushes in that. They scrubbed their teeth and then thinned the mixture in their mouths with saliva to make it easier to swallow because they weren't allowed to spit it out. Then the maid came down the line with another jam jar of water so the girls could dip their brushes in to rinse them.

The girls ate in the back yard. There was a long table, and benches. If the benches were too wet to sit on, they ate standing up, bending to the food so as not to let it drop. Two lines of girls standing facing each other across the wet table bowing like a grotesque parody of some Far Eastern ritual. When it was raining they stood in line along the house wall to eat, under the verandah.

The maids were allowed no opportunity to go out with men. The girls never saw any boys. One day, when my mother was on duty cleaning the dormitory, a maid took her to a small attic bedroom. There were no personal bits and pieces even there. It was as bare as a cell. The maid, who seemed a grown-up to the little girl, a grown-up of sixteen or seventeen, laid her plump body on the bed and pulled up her clothes exposing her flesh, flabby from a poor diet. My mother had never seen pubic hair before. It crouched, black, between the maid's thighs, like a spider.

My mother was made to 'do things' to the maid. Had to stroke the spider. The maid writhed on the narrow cot, her eyes opening in panic or anger if my mother's fingers stopped their probing. A large puffy hand closed over her smaller one and forced it into a rhythmic pattern of movement. The maid's eyes closed, her body went rigid, and she let out a series of hoarse moans. It seemed to my mother that the maid was in terrible pain. That was the only lesson in love-making given to those children who had never been loved.

My mother would grow into a woman who could never associate sex with love. What else could you expect? She went away and hid, from the horror, the shame, the fear. No one was ever told. She grew, loathing her body. Saw hair grow on it like fungus on dead wood. She wore hate like armour. Used it like a knife.

One night a man came into the girls' dormitory. He came in unsteadily via the fire exit, wearing a trilby hat far back on his head. 'Hil'ry! Hil'ry!' His voice was slurred, hoarse, urgent. The dormitory was dark. The whispering stopped. It was silent except for the breathing of the girls already asleep. 'Hil'ry!'

One girl sat up in bed. 'Daddy?'

'My li'l girl.'

He moved erratically into a pool of moonlight. His suit was crumpled. His trousers seemed two sizes too large. Hilary slid out of bed and ran across the floor. He staggered as she threw her arms round him. He swayed, as she clung onto him, like a tree in a high wind. She appeared to be propping him up. The girls stared (the girls who were never held) watching the strange spectacle.

'I'm going take you 'way,' he said.

But the maids came. And the sisters. The girls saw Hilary, distraught and tearful, dragged off. They watched the women maul and manhandle the drunk out of the room as he called to his daughter in maudlin terms making promises which melted on his breath as he mouthed them. Hustled away, he was forbidden to visit his child again. But the strange scene in the moonlight was not forgotten. The girls dreamt of the man who would come to free them. But they had been sentenced for life and their prisons were impregnable. They despised the man too because he was not man enough.

My mother finished school at fourteen. She had no childish things to put away. (They weren't allowed.) She had been trained to scrub floors, scour pans, and be subservient. She went to work as a kitchen maid for a lord and lady in London. And when they went back to their country seat in Ulster, she was bundled off like the rest of their baggage. She was allowed out one afternoon a week. A brief taste of freedom from the drudgery of the kitchen. A time to walk unfettered and to breathe untrammelled air. Her movements were followed by the eyes of village boys who mentally stripped her, feeling the iron hardness of their new weapons. My father was among them, his eyes cold, blue, penetrating.

He was an illegitimate child in a land in the pincer grip of vice-like religions. He never saw his mother. Never sucked from her. He was expelled like garbage and carted away. He was fostered by Mrs Greig, the matriarchal driving force of a small farm. Her family scrabbled in the cold earth for a livelihood, fighting against the bitter climate, at war with the soil. Her virtue was not peasant warmth, but small-farm grit and flint. Little John brought a little cash, paid out of secret guilt. But the money was tainted. The child was dirty. Grew, fit for the dirty work. Grew, with a dirty mind. (What else could you expect?) Grew, and withdrew behind scaly armouring. Grew hard with hate and cold without love.

The local boys were peasant stock. Short. Sturdy. Bovine. Slow. John grew tall and lean. Quick as an assassin's thrust. Cold as anaesthetic. As sharp as the point of a hypodermic syringe. My parents were drawn together. He jabbed. She was numbed. Felt the pain of his prick. Felt him empty his icy hatred into her dead body. More of a wrestle than an embrace, they were locked together from the first moment they lay on the frost-hard earth. Both needing warmth. Needing a home that neither of them had ever known.

Seventeen and pregnant, she married. They moved into half a room in the Greigs' house. A partition was put up to divide the second bedroom. My mother tried to learn the work of the farm. Her young husband rode the cart. She forked up hay, rapping his ankles. He swore. She rapped his ankles again and again, working against time as the cloud banks built up across the Ulster sky and the hay lay at the mercy of the coming rain. Her hands were blistered and bleeding. Her back and arms ached like labour. The hay fork was heavy and unwieldy. She rapped his ankles repeatedly until he jumped down and beat her in the field.

Out of that dead union came a child. My brother Peter was born with pain. My mother hated her body; hated the swelling; hated the dirt that came out of her, the blood and mess. Instead of *giving* birth, she fought it. And it tore her. She hated her husband (who found other flesh to use) and hated her baby son.

The child was cared for in a rough and ready sort of way by old Mrs Greig. (A farmer's concern for livestock.) My mother was fucked regularly in cold contempt. And inseminated again. Mrs Greig's son, Sammy, found the fighting too noisy through the partition (the swearing, screaming, scuffling, slapping, and crying, and then the rhythmic rattling of the bed). John and his thin, ailing, alien wife were moved out to the Nissen hut some way from the house. A new home. A new prison. Where I was born. Nine months imprisoned inside a dead uterus. Dragged out into a dead world. A sickly child of sick parents. I drew the milk from my mother's breast and threw up. Spewed up everything she gave me. I could keep down milk from only one cow: not one of the Greigs', but one of McClintock's. It was as though nature in her wisdom was trying to kill me but God in his malice was trying to keep me alive.

My mother, not yet out of her teens, was weak and ill, despised by the tough peasant family. Useless on the land, she was made to slave in the scullery. My father, a lad still, as desperate for love as a trapped pitman for air, went searching into the evening after sweating from dawn, seeking his mother in the young bodies of local girls. Demanding a mother's love. Punishing them for not providing it. Fucking his thin unloving wife when he could find nothing better.

The rain battered on the corrugated iron roof of the Nissen hut. The icy needles of the Ulster rain colder even than the back-yard rain of the girl's childhood. The young mother nursed her loneliness in the dim cell, without warmth. With no warmth for the two brats, whining and sleepless, or the third now in the dead prison of her womb. She sat among the scruffy muddle of their sparse possessions wanting and not wanting him to come home to where she waited alone and cold and crying out for comfort. And he came locked inside himself. Resentful, defensive, each battered against the shell of the other like rain against the Nissen hut roof. Cold hulks clashing together like warships colliding in an arctic sea. Their business, destruction. Their motivation, revenge.

They came together looking for love, but neither had learned to love. Each demanding the impossible, but neither with anything to give. Both felt betrayed and rejected yet again. They retreated further inside themselves like vulnerable animals trying to find a snug safe place to hibernate from the hurtful wintry world. During the day my father fought with the wind and the rain, the sun and the earth, the beasts and the Greigs. In the evening he fought with the local girls who tried to resist. At night he fought with his wife. Stumbling around in their dingy oil-lit confinement, sweeping the screaming children aside, they slapped, and scratched, and swore, and fucked.

During the war they tried to escape from everything that was behind them. Terrified of the German submarines they crossed the Irish sea. In England there was a shortage of farm workers. (Colonising countries have always been greedy for the man-power of their colonies when it suited their needs.) They moved into a farm labourer's cottage in Essex. She lay in the contortions of her third labour while he ravished a land girl in the next room. (A land girl who had come to help with the delivery.) When the girl discovered she was pregnant my father cleared out. Us children went to foster homes. My mother found herself a job in a factory. My father went to work in the docks and shacked up with another woman. He took back his eldest son and his baby daughter. But he never came for me. Later an ulcer burst in his stomach while he was working. Poison from the rottenness that was in him spread through his

111

body. Before the ambulance reached the hospital he was dead. (He died at an early age.) His children were sent to Barnardo's homes.

On the day they were coming to take Josephine I stayed off work. Laura got up that morning and made herself ready while I dressed the baby and gave her breakfast. Then I sat with her on the settee. I kept placing a plastic cup on my head and every time it slid off onto the seat between us she laughed. Laura sat on the arm of a chair playing the guitar I'd bought her for her birthday, singing snatches of songs. *I could have loved you better, didn't mean to be unkind, you know that was the last thing on my mind.* A car stopped outside. I picked Jo up and walked to the window. The sun was shining brilliantly onto the other side of the street. The car stood in ominous shadow. A man in a grey suit got out of the offside and walked round to the pavement. He held the door open for a woman in a black dress and brown cardigan. They exchanged words looking at the house, and then the woman passed out of my sight towards the front door. The man leaned back against the bonnet and folded his arms. He looked like a plainclothes policeman. The knock sounded in my head like the slamming of a punishment cell door.

Laura leaned the guitar against the side of her chair and stood up. The guitar fell leaving a strange discordant sound shuddering in the air as she went out of the room. I held Jo tight against my chest and kissed her face and hand. 'Jo, Jo. I love you. I'm not sending you away because I don't love you, but because I do. You won't be able to understand that, but I want you to have a good mummy and daddy who'll take care of you. I want you to have a nice home – not a shithouse like this. They'll take you somewhere nice, Jo, to people who'll love you. I'm sorry, Jo. I'm sorry.'

They were climbing the stairs like executioners, their voices relaxed and calm. The woman introduced herself and then took Jo from me. Jo started to cry and reached out her arms to me but the woman held onto her with the firmness and self-

113

assurance of a court official. The woman addressed the baby for a while in an artificial way. Then, turning to us, she went over the adoption procedure again in a daft sing-song sort of voice like those women on the wireless who tell kids to be leaves or something while someone tinkles on a piano. Then, carrying my little daughter, she turned and walked out of the door.

The children's home I was sent to when I was five was a Dickensian leftover located in the Gothic horror of a huge Victorian house. Its grey-black asphalt yard was entombed by tall grey-brick walls. We boys ate in the yard, unless the weather was too bad. Miss Batt was the governor. She was six feet tall, built like an obelisk. She had white hair and her moustache was white except where black hairs sprouted from moles. She wore a large size in men's flat brown shoes and a blue wiry suit, as spiky as a cactus. She stood on the ground as cold and immovable as a ship's bollard on the dockside. Miss Thorne was chief screw. Her body was short and stubby belying the sharp spite of her temper. She had iron-grey hair and an iron will. Her only physical contact with us kids was through ruler or cane. There were no maids. We were the skivvies. The bigger inmates looked after the smaller ones. And bullied them. What else could you expect? Miss Batt and her accomplice bullied us all.

The Victorians seemed able to design houses so that the windows never let in any light. The schoolroom was as dingy and dusty as an underground dungeon. By the time I was six I could say the days of the week and the months of the year backwards in French. (I never learned to speak French.) There were no desks. We sat on long benches – cold rows of ridiculously forlorn knobby white knees. When we were not using our sticks of chalk we had to sit with our hands, vulnerable as victims of a rape, on our slates. A long ruler lay between Miss Batt's thighs, or sometimes she held it erect on her lap. She used it to point at the blackboard or a wall chart as we chanted our tables or alphabet. She used it to point at a child whom she wanted to answer a question. Looking down the length of the ruler was like looking into the muzzle of a firing squad rifle. Our thoughts petrified into a black O. The power of speech deserted us. For saying nothing as well as for speaking out of turn, or a spoken or written mistake, the ruler cracked across our knuckles.

Beside each bed in the dismal dormitory was a small cupboard for our clothes. In the bottom of the cupboard was a shoe box where we kept our toys. Anything that wouldn't fit was taken away. The toys could be played with only on Saturday afternoons, outside in the prison yard – weather permitting.

Those days and nights merge indistinguishably in my memory with only a few incidents painfully clear, like fingertips cut to the bone. It was like waking erratically from a bad dream remembering only the most recent incident – the one that woke you – then being dragged down into disturbed sleep as the nightmare reclaims you. It was like being caught on the moors by black night and curling fog that swirls around the terrors that taunt you while wet bog sucks and clings at your frightened feet making flight impossible.

I remember my mother visiting. It was a Saturday afternoon. There was a man with her who stood in shadow. My mother told me it had been my birthday some days before, which meant I was six. She gave me a toy car made of tin, a police car painted black and white. After she left (Miss Batt didn't like visitors to linger too long – it upset the other boys, she said) I ran around in the grey yard pulling the police car behind me on a piece of string. A boy, racing the other way in a game of his own, trampled on the car. The asphalt was transformed from race track to scrap yard. The police car was an irreparable wreck. I started to cry. Miss Thorne came. Crying wasn't allowed.

Somewhere in that nightmare I caught whooping cough. One night, coughing and unable to catch my breath, I was sick on the sheet. When Miss Batt came on her nightly round she found me, still whooping and coughing, in my sick bed. She dragged me out and hit me twice about the head. She told me to strip the sheet from the bed and take it to the laundry room. When I came back she was waiting with the cane.

Somewhere in that remorseless dream I began to wet the bed. Every night Miss Batt would wake me and abuse me. I was a filthy, offensive and abominable beast. I didn't deserve the privilege of a place in the home but should have been flung back like garbage into the gutter where I belonged. She made me take the wet-heavy sheets to the laundry room and then I was caned. I spent the rest of the night on the rubber undersheet. if the urine soaked into the mattress, Miss Thorne would make me piss in a chamber pot the following morning, and drink the piss.

I don't remember where we went, or why, but sometimes we would walk in twos through streets outside those dark enclosing walls. Once in an escape attempt I tried to board a passing bus. It was a double-decker with a platform at the back. I got hold of the handrail as the bus gathered speed, lost balance and was dragged like a sack of old rags along the road. I didn't release my grip but the conductor kept ringing the bell until the bus came to a standstill. Lacerated and humiliated I was returned to captivity and correction.

On a forced march through the town during my second bout of whooping cough I collapsed. With my face pressed against the cold bosom of the pavement I retched and gasped and gagged. I prayed for death to gather me up in its black cloak. Instead I was wrapped in a grey hospital blanket. I tasted jelly and ice-cream. Then I was collected by my mother. She was as much a stranger to me as I must have been to her.

Sophie was born here in this rented house in a strange town, yet with very little money Sheila made it a home. Sophie was kept clean and cared for and chubby with good food, but Sheila's composure was precarious, seemingly always on a knife-edge. She repeatedly overbalanced and broke down, screaming for up to an hour without respite. I didn't know how to handle it. I used to put Sophie in the pram and take her for long walks trying to keep her out of reach of the disturbance until Sheila had calmed down. The frequency of these fits increased until they were occurring every few days.

The only people we knew here were my old school friend and his wife. But when this section of the motorway was completed Bud was moved away to another site. Next door there's a fat widow who's forever bawling at her three boys in the back room (the eldest has just joined the army so that he can get bawled at for the rest of his life). She's called Aunty Doris to her face, the Street Newspaper behind her back. She's the sort who will do anything for you – whether you like it or not. Our neighbours on the other side pretend we don't exist. They're respectable working-class. Their son is thirty-five and still lives at home with his mum and dad. Father and son work in the same mill and they vote Tory. The Indian people are a closed community. Occasionally one of them is cornered on his own and beaten up to show that we're more civilised than them. Most of the white families are on the dole or social welfare. There's a bit of villainy going on among the dads and vandalism among the lads. Parents are always slapping or belting their children. The kids bash each other, the bigger ones battering the smaller. Several of the men and women are alcoholics, sending the kids down the shop for booze. A third of the families have only one parent. None of the houses have gardens. Most of the houses have dogs and cats. Several pets

118

have been turned out to live, scavenging, on the street. When the woman opposite was deserted, she took the kids to her mother's for five weeks. She left the dog in the locked house. It starved to death. The neighbours heard it whimpering – but did nothing.

The kids live on a diet of meat pie and chips, sweets and crisps. The teenage girls and young wives are pale and spotty and overweight. Their eyes are listless. Their hair is lifeless. They have no future. There's only one attractive woman in the street. Because she bleaches her hair Sheila thought she was a tart.

Sheila went to a pottery course two mornings a week. She enjoyed the classes and I enjoyed having the time on my own with Sophie. The pressure seemed to go with Sheila out of the house. I'd play with the baby, sing to her, bath her, feed her. The only part of caring for her I didn't like was changing shitty nappies. I tried to avoid breathing in the sickly smell and getting the milky shit on my hands.

Sheila wanted me to go to a class. But I couldn't find anything I was interested in.

I used to go out walking. Sometimes with Sophie. Often alone. I found that if I went along the canal towpath I could be out of town within a few minutes. About a mile from the top of our street a cattle bridge leads into a meadow. On the far side there's a wooded rise, and beyond that a valley has been scored out by a stream. It was a little piece of paradise – a far remove from the ugliness of civilisation. In all the times I went there unaccompanied I never saw or heard another person.

I first discovered it one day in February. I could hear the stream long before I could see it. Then, between the dead, still grey of the trees I glimpsed the live, turbulent grey of the water. Its song was like the sound of steady pouring rain. At first I wasn't aware of the birds but once my ear became attuned I realised the air was always vibrant with their voices. From among the miscellany I isolated a skylark. I looked up, straining my eyes, but couldn't locate it. The sky was pigeon-grey and dove-white, with a patch of blue at its throat. Distant traffic rumbled like a beast murmuring in its sleep.

I stood still on top of the hill. The winter trees were as bare and dead-looking as stacked kindling. But then, startlingly, I saw the colours. The trees were an astonishing moss-green. I'd always thought they were just plain brown, as in a child's picture. I felt like a kitten, a few days old, whose eyes were beginning to open, who was able to look around in surprise at this world full of colour that had only been heard and smelt but never seen. And yet I was twenty years old. What had they done to me that my eyes were only now starting to open?

I looked around like someone who's just had cataracts removed. Tumbled stones from a long disused dry-stone wall were scattered on the ground clothed in the same green as the trees. Evergreen ivy, in a different shade, with its delicately patterned leaves, dark green on rich brown, clung to some of the trees like a lover, its arms round the loved one's neck, its feelers at the loved one's throat. Grass was a paler green near its roots, but yellow on top like bleached hair. Tattered remnants of last year's leaves were fawn, or orangy-brown like the bracken. Turning, I saw that the trunks on their south-facing sides were a less vivid green with speckled-grey breasts. Sheltered branches nestled, shining, brown and grey. A dead stump, almost black, was alive with grass and weed and moss in a dozen different shades and patterns. Bramble, bracken, fern, and grass protectively enveloped a fallen tree. Old bramble leaves, as well chewed as an old tomcat's ears, were still partly green, bordered with brown.

Some trunks were as pitted as a rock-face, with vertical cracks. On others the cracks were horizontal and the trunks knotted. Others again were smooth-barked and silver-grey, as tall as a six-storey building. Many had branches only at the very top so that each one looked like a spray of flowers in an elegantly tall vase. The tops of the trees in the valley were level with the tops of the shorter trees on the hill as though they had agreed to share equally the light.

The trunk of one tree twisted around itself like a skein of wool. Another was tall, slim, and graceful, yet its base was swollen, gnarled, deformed, harbouring black water in an ugly pit. I wondered how such beauty could have grown from such a beginning. Another tree had a family of four equal trunks springing from a single base. On one tree a single orange leaf was left quivering in a wind too gentle for me to feel. A young sapling stood proud and strong in its youth, untouched by moss or lichen. Half the trees were dead. A branch broke off at a touch without resistance. A cracked bough hung down to the ground, the exposed interior as yellow and soft as a sponge cake. An eight-foot trunk, as bare as a Greek column, stood like the final remnant of a ruined temple.

A million buds stood erect and proud in their small swelling. Some were fat-round and green. Others spear-like and brown. And, sometimes, death and life on a single branch.

A dry-stone wall marked the frontier between the anaemic grass of the forest floor and the vigorous green of pasture. A distant pylon was the only evidence that I hadn't stepped into the past. I started to stroll down to the stream and my feet slid in the damp leaf-mould. The dry crack of snapping twigs mingled with the wet squish of mud. A bramble stood sturdily across my path like the arm of a level-crossing barrier. Away in the field, a sheep, as still as on an outcrop of stone, studied my distant movement.

I made my way carefully down the steep slope taking my weight on the front of my foot, reaching toes for root and rock. I ran three quick steps and fell against the buffer of a green trunk. A few rusty springs from a long-ago bed lay at the base, reaching for my ankles. Down further, where the previous year's lank blond grass hung down like unkempt hair, my foot suddenly slid forward from under me. I put out my hand to break my fall. My hand was damp, flecked brown with leaf-mould turning to earth. I left a patterned skid mark on the soil.

On the stream bank I found a natural boomerang — the bare wood almost ginger; a large piece of curved black bark, like an abandoned mudguard; a twisted branch, not yet completely naked — a snake fossilized in the act of shedding its skin. I squatted and carressed with my fingertips a silk-smooth stick, the palest fawn with here and there a delicate tracery of grey-green. As I straightened up, a hanging twig caught like an insect in my hair, startling me.

I stood by the curling stream and watched it writhing noisily to join another. They married and flowed on as one. A tree grew isolated in the middle of the water course, roots exposed above an elongated sand bar so that it appeared to be on stilts. Rocks littered the stream bed, darker green and darker grey than on the earth, almost black. Moss grew on the stone above the level of the water. As well as rocks, fallen trees, even a tyre impeded the flow, but the drive of the water was irresistible. One small channel broke away from the main stream, finding its own short cut, and rejoined its parent later. The water was a dark browny-green upstream. Downstream it was black, flecked with the white crests of tiny waves.

I looked up again at the sky. There was a bright patch of silver-grey, where the sun lay behind the cloud, like a light seen through a glass shade. Beyond the cloud, blue sky was spreading, fading to a paler blue towards the horizon. Then the curtain of cloud parted and the upper sections of some of the trunks glowed silvery-white, and the sprayed treetops changed to orange from black. In the pasture the weak sun washed over the gentle swelling mounds of winter green with their bassets of grey, while black shadows like iron bars and steel mesh patterned the forest floor.

I felt at peace. The tension that accompanied every minute of waking life with Sheila was washed away by stream and trees and earth, and the noisy silence of this sanctuary.

I went back there, desperate for narcosis, over and over again.

I was shopping with Sophie when the good-looking woman from over the road came into the Co-op with her little boy. She had him on a lead, as if he were a dog. There were no other customers in the shop and on impulse I asked her if I could see her sometime. We could have been Mr and Mrs Average, with our regulation-issue little boy and baby girl, discussing among the shelves whether or not to get an extra packet of frozen peas while they were on special offer and we could save five pence on our next purchase.

'It's difficult,' Sharon said. She didn't look surprised. It was as if she had been expecting me to ask.

'What about this afternoon?'

'Where? Folk talk.' The little lad got hold of a can of ravioli and the tower of tins rocked. She jerked him away with the reins and slapped his hand. His face crumpled and he cried. It made me feel like slapping her.

'Along the canal,' I said.

'Whereabouts?'

'Out of town towards the aqueduct there's a cattle bridge.'

'All right. I can leave this one with my mother, but I've to be back before t'others get home from school.'

'Two o'clock?'

'All right.'

We stumbled across the field to the wood. The pasture was uneven and the hollows sodden. I felt the wet seeping into my socks inside my plimsolls. Under the trees the earth was firmer but slippery. She was wearing ridiculous shoes and I used this excuse to put my arm round her. She was a good-looking blonde with blue eyes, although her hair was as dark at the roots as her eyebrows. There was something about her mouth. Her mouth was resentful. We hardly spoke. I fucked her up against a tree studying the subtlety of colour and texture in the moss on the trunk. While she put her pants back on I looked around the bit of scrubby woodland I had thought of as paradise. The sin wasn't sex, but the lack of caring. We arranged to meet the following Thursday. It became a weekly event. We met. Fucked. Separated. And the rest of the week ignored each other on the street where we lived.

From when I went to live with my mother at the age of six I was, in a sense, a model child. I played the Perfect Wife to my mother's Victorian Husband; doing the housework, submitting passively to brutality, asking for nothing, endeavouring to earn a little love while the resentment inside me grew and festered like an ulcer. I came home from schools that I detested to dismal, damp, untidy, cold rooms that I loathed. I got the coal in. Chopped wood. Lit the fire. Tidied up. Made the beds. Put a flame to the gas light. Washed up the breakfast things. Made the tea and laid the table.

On Saturdays I dusted and polished and did the shopping. When we still had rationing she used to sell the sweet and clothing coupons so there was money for cheese and eggs. But there was never enough to eat.

She had a white trench coat. She pinched pennies for weeks to get it cleaned. She collected it from the cleaner's one evening on the way home from work and hung it on the back of the living room door. I'd forgotten to put margarine on the table. She went to the corner cupboard where the food was kept while I cut bread. I'd been hungry when I'd come in from school. I'd eaten some currants. She squatted in the corner looking into the cupboard, motionless for a moment. Although there was no-where I could run I began to move away from her, slowly, silently, backing towards the door. She picked a currant off the floor and peered at it like a monkey that has found a flea in its fur. Still squatting, she twisted towards me, loathsome as a toad. 'Have you been stealing currants?'

'No.'

'Have you been stealing currants? I said.'

'No.'

'No, what?'

'No, Mum.'

Her voice was as hard and cold as the steel cutting edge of a guillotine. She nailed me to the floor with eyes of hatred. 'Don't lie to me.' Her voice was beginning to rise in a countdown to the hysterical outburst I knew was imminent. 'Tell me the truth. Have you been stealing currants?'

There was no movement in the room. No sign of life. A stone predator stonily eyeing its stone prey. 'No.'

Her eyes unpinned me as she twisted her face away. She took a packet of white lard from the cupboard, and as she turned and rose, spiralling up and forward, hurled it at me. I ducked. It hit my head, bursting and splattering in my hair, and thudded against the sleeve of the newly cleaned coat on the door. With a scream of anguish she sprang like a cougar across the room and hit me about the head and face until I fell. She hauled me up and holding me by the hair began bashing my face against the wall. I felt the bone crunch in my nose. My nose and lips were bleeding, the blood bitter and frightening in my mouth. She let me go and sank onto the brown oval tin box that was our fireside chair threatening that if I didn't stop crying she would hit me again. The broken bone was never set. The gash was never stitched. She didn't want anyone to know.

Sheila came home from her pottery classes later and later. One Thursday she'd come in particularly late. We were sitting at the table having eaten, drinking mugs of tea. It was sunny outside, but the spring sun didn't rise high enough to clear the factory wall so the living room was dim and the yard in shadow. There was a strong vinegary smell from the lino works.

She put down her mug and peered into it. 'I've just slept with Roger,' she said. Roger was the pottery teacher.

I stared at her bowed head. Her hands were shaking, her fingertips pressed against the mug to steady them. A jagged pulse of pain passed through me, followed by calm. 'You must've been tired.'

She looked at me, frowning. 'What?'

I sighed. 'You must've been tired. To sleep with him. Why didn't you fuck him?'

'You know what I mean.'

'Yeah.'

'Well?'

'Well what?'

'Is that all you've got to say?'

I shrugged and looked out of the window. I could see black smudges of soot settling on the nappies on the line. It seemed impossible to keep anything clean and unspoiled. 'It's up to you who you sleep with.'

'I thought you might be angry.'

'Why should I be angry?'

'Well, you might be hurt.'

The man from next door rode up the back alley. He dismounted and wheeled his bike into the yard. I suddenly realised he must have come off the two o'clock shift and that I should be meeting Sharon. I got up from the table. 'I'm going out for a walk.'

128

'Are you all right?' She stood up. Hesitated. She couldn't decide whether to put her arms round me or not.

'Sure.' I kissed her. She clung onto me. I felt trapped. I wanted to get away. 'I think I can hear the baby,' I said.

We kissed again and then she went upstairs and I went out. I walked fast and the walking seemed to release the pain from wherever I'd pushed it to and it flowed through me. It was like a hunger pain. Terrible hunger.

Sharon was waiting by the bridge. She looked pleased to see me. 'I thought you weren't coming.' she said.

'I'm feeling sadistic,' I said, 'so if you don't want to come you'd better go back now.'

She looked scared and excited. I led her across the field gripping the back of her neck. We walked hurriedly up the hill and through the wood, tripping occasionally over bramble or dead wood. I was trembling. I kissed her viciously, holding her by the hair. I could hear the stream, and birds singing, and a faint tractor a long way off. Sunshine splattered through the trees like blood.

I stripped her naked, tearing her underclothes. I unbuckled my belt and pulled it through the loops of my jeans. When she saw what I was doing her eyes widened in fear. She said, 'No,' once, but didn't move, like a mouse paralysed by the sight of a snake.

I strapped her then. Not hard. I wanted to hurt – but I didn't want to hurt *her*. I felt the impulse to thrash and thrash until I was exhausted, as my mother had done so many times to me – but I held back. I strapped her, and then I fucked her. And afterwards I was overwhelmed by a feeling of tenderness towards her. Concern and sorrow and pity filled me to overflowing, and I held her close to comfort her, vainly wishing the fullness of my feelings could permeate her affection-starved body.

I walked along by the canal. Not used commercially any more, the banks had been allowed to cave in. The reeds and weeds which encroached across the waterway, the newly arrived swallows, dipping, swooping, skimming its surface, the pair of swans, proud squatters who had made their home there – all gave it the appearance of a natural place. Nearer the town it was used as a rubbish dump, and prams, car tyres, bicycle frames and mattresses were only half hidden by the dirty water.

I felt confused about many things. What demon was it that drove me to thrash Sharon? How could I use the pity I felt when I perceived her as victim and identified with her pain? Was it my mother I wanted to hurt? Or Sheila? I had loved Sheila as I'd never loved anyone before. But this disturbed person I lived with wasn't the sad and beautiful woman whose hair I'd stroked across a green carpet. Only two things bound me to her now: fear of being left alone; and our baby daughter who was growing more important to me every day. I carried two memories always with me: my mother leaving; and someone taking my little girl away.

I was anxious when I got home but Sheila greeted me inside the front door with a smile. She held her arms open. 'Hello, darling,' she said. 'I'm so glad you're back.' She pressed her arms round me and crushed her mouth onto mine and I relaxed into her warmth. Then she held her head back to look into my face and her expression had changed. The welcoming smile had gone. I felt a cold clutch of fear. I could feel myself withdrawing. Diminishing. Becoming a child again. My shell hardening.

She said, 'You've been with a woman.' I looked defiantly into her eyes but said nothing. 'Haven't you?' A dozen different answers dashed through my mind, but none could say all I needed to say, and besides a barrier had banged shut between my brain and my throat. She let go of me and stepped back a pace. 'Why don't you answer?' I felt trapped and the snare grew taut around my neck and limbs. 'Have you?' she screamed. 'Have you been with a woman?' Her voice was a hammer that beat me further into myself and turned me to stone.

'I know you have. I can smell it on you. You've got a woman, haven't you? Why are you so secretive about it? Why? Why won't you tell me? Don't just stand there like a guilty little boy. Why are you so deceitful? I don't care if you've been with a woman. Why can't you just be honest? That's all. I'm honest with you. Aren't I? Aren't I?' I couldn't bear to look at her face any more. Her skin was white and tight, her eyes as large as a Belsen survivor's, burning as bright as the eyes of a victim of a tropical disease. She looked like a mad woman as she spat out words like poison darts. 'Go on. Admit it. I can smell it on you. You stink of her.'

I saw her grief as clearly as an open wound and I wanted to encompass her in the comfort of my arms. But the life blood had left me – I was a robot whose motor was programmed to switch off when it registered overload. I wanted to say that I was sorry; that I didn't want to hurt her; that I ached for the comfort of a woman's body every moment of the day and night; that I felt driven to try to conquer sexually every woman I could; that I was afraid. But no words came.

Life is a set of Chinese boxes. To escape from one prison is to find yourself in the next.

Eventually, to liberate herself from a life sentence of loneliness and poverty, my mother married a weak, ineffectual man called Claude whom she didn't like. Claude was an orphan who'd left school and retreated into the anonymity and security of the army. After twenty-five years he had risen to the dizzy heights of pay clerk with the rank of sergeant. On civvy street at fifty, and still a junior clerk, he was picked up by my mother, the way a mouse is picked up by a cat, and suddenly found himself with a depressive and domineering young wife who despised him, and a strange and silent self-contained boy withdrawn to some secluded defended place beyond reach, who ignored him.

Claude, anxious to please my mother, gradually eased the load from my back. She would come home from work and sit with her feet in the grate, her stockings rolled down around swollen ankles, varicose veins standing out like knotted purple cord in legs mottled red from exposure to the heat. Claude came home and pottered till after midnight, working unceasingly, slowly and inefficiently.

She bullied us both. Some nights I was too scared to sleep. I had this fear that she might bash my head in with a hammer while I was unprotected. I would lie in bed straining to keep sore eyelids from sagging while dread dragged my belly like a dredger at work on a river bed. I would hold my breath, hearing her voice, like claws, hurting Claude in the next room. I prayed passionately, 'Dear God, please kill her in the night so I don't have to live with her any more.' But God was either dead or deaf or a bigger bastard than she was.

When I was fourteen she put down a deposit on a new bungalow. It had a bathroom with a real bath. I had a room of

132

my own. A place at last to be alone. The garden was a building site, a rubble of concrete and bricks. She'd dreamed of a garden ever since she'd been imprisoned behind high walls in the drab grey yard of her childhood. She wanted instant flowering fertility. She ordered turf for a square lawn. Bought plants to stand like prison guards uniformly spaced around the perimeter. Claude took over as houseboy, while I was sent to struggle resentfully with the strange elements outside. I broke a spade and two forks and dug up the sewage pipe. She watched from the lounge window, as from a prison tower, and fumed and bitched. The turf died before it was laid. The plants withered.

In my last year of school the police picked up my brother for vagrancy, and contacted my mother. They informed her that my father was dead. I went with her on a bus to another town to collect Peter, excited at the prospect of having a big brother. He turned out to be a flabby, pasty-faced lad of sixteen with pale blue eyes and a pathetic angelic look. Polio had left him with a limp which became more severe whenever he smelled sympathy. When we first met him the limp was very bad indeed. We moved another single bed into my room and I emptied half the drawers in my chest. He had nothing to put in them.

Peter got a job as a pig-man and tried desperately to please his mother. In his attempts to ingratiate himself he relieved me of many duties, such as the nauseating task of pulling the grey hairs from her head. When he brushed her hair he followed through each downward stroke sliding his hand across her breast. This ritual took place nightly for several weeks until one day, tense and irritated, she turned on him like a pet alsatian suddenly savaging the master's child, and the shaky structure of hope and fantasy he was building was demolished like a toddler's tower of toy bricks.

She usually undressed in the living room in front of us all, but because of the way Peter leered at her she began to undress in her bedroom. One night she heard a noise and surprised Peter at the keyhole. She tried to goad Claude into hitting him, but Claude couldn't do it.

Peter clearly felt himself to be in competition with Claude and myself for my mother's favour. I wasn't playing, but Peter kept ending up a loser anyway. He constantly volunteered to do

133

things in order to please her, but she was never satisfied with anything anybody did and he invariably earned criticism instead of praise. He was ready to crawl on his belly or wallow in pig-swill for her affection, and she despised him for it. There was no fatted calf brought out for this prodigal son.

To make matters worse, Peter had another rival. Gerry worked in the same shop as my mother. He took her to work in his car mornings, brought her home at night, and was teaching her to drive on their afternoons off. I had seen my mother relating to men often enough to know they were having an affair. But that was their business.

Peter followed me into the kitchen. He leaned against the sink watching me as I took a slice of bread from the packet. The marge had been left out, a knife sticking into it like a dagger in a murder victim's back. The jam pot was practically empty. I scraped the sides thoroughly and collected a mound of red gunge in the bottom. I scooped it all onto the bread, aware of Peter's watchfulness, wondering whether he would tell my mother that I'd taken too much.

'I saw Mum and Gerry this afternoon,' he said. I raised my eyebrows in reply. I wondered what he expected me to say. 'They were on the common in Gerry's car.' The thin slice began to tear under the weight of jam as I bit into it. Peter watched me as intently as a cat stalking a bird. 'He was doing things to her,' he said. He hadn't begun to shave but soft blond bum-fluff was sprouting repulsively on his face. 'You know,' he went on, 'having sex. Doing her.' He made a circle with forefinger and thumb and poked his other forefinger in and out. I crammed the remainder of the slice in my mouth and shrugged. Peter moved against me and I had to steel myself not to draw away from the physical contact. He spoke in a stage whisper. 'Do you think we should tell Claude?'

I moved away, wiping my fingers on the back of my trousers. 'No.'

'Do you believe me?'

I shrugged again. 'If you say so.'

I didn't care one way or the other. I went out to work on the garden. I hated getting my hands dirty. Hated the filth up my finger nails. But she made me do things to it. She got crazes. She'd decided she wanted a rockery. She'd probably seen one in someone else's garden or in a woman's magazine. I was digging up one corner of the lawn and humping earth and stones to build a hill. I was still at it when she came home.

Claude came in soon after. It was beginning to get dark. She called me from the back door. I could hear from the tightness of her voice that there was trouble. My insides seemed to be dropping out of me like diarrhoea. I sighed and let go of the rock I was rolling to the rockery. It tipped back and settled on the lawn. I felt cold under my sweat and shivered. I went in slowly, rubbing my hands together so that the earth crumbled.

I went through the kitchen and into the living room – the room she called the lounge. The light was on and the curtains closed. Her face was pale and her lips compressed and almost colourless. Her eyes were wide and staring giving her a slightly demented look. 'Come here!' Peter was standing to one side of her. He seemed frightened. Claude was hovering in a corner looking wretched and miserable. He was stooped as though trying to become small. I went and stood in front of her. She licked her lips with a quick movement like a lizard catching an insect. 'What have you been saying to Peter?' I glanced at his anxious face then gazed down at the carpet. 'Answer me!'

There was silence in the room. I could hear the alarm clock on the mantelpiece and my mother's breathing. No one moved. 'What have you been saying?' They had the radio on next door. Then their baby began to cry. She cried, just as every baby that has ever been born has cried, for somebody to come. She found herself alone, with the people she loved out of sight and feared they would never come back. So she howled aloud her need for attention and bodily comfort, expressing not only her desire to be loved but demanding physical proof. But no one went to her, and I could feel the tears forming in my eyes.

'Answer me when I speak to you!' my mother said. 'What did you say?' I felt as if I was shrinking, like Alice in Nightmare- land. I retreated further inside, closing doors after me as I went. I felt myself to be like a set of those dolls that fit one inside the other, and I made my way to the middle. I became the very smallest, the one that no one can open, the one with nothing inside. All that stood in the room was a wooden replica of myself.

'What did you say?'

'Nothing.'

It was obvious I knew what she was talking about. Her eyes squinted now into narrow slits. Her rage narrowed onto its target.

'Did you tell him you'd seen me with Gerry?'

'No.'

She turned on Peter. 'Did he?'

'Yes, Mum.'

I stared at the carpet, hearing the voices muffled, like hammer blows on the nails of my coffin lid.

'Did he?' she repeated.

'Yes, Mum.'

'Are you sure?'

'Yes, Mum.'

'I'm going to get to the bottom of this. Paul. Look at me. Paul!' I looked at my shoes caked in mud. I was supposed to take them off at the kitchen door. 'What did you say about me?'

'Nothing.'

'One of you's lying. Now which is it? Are you telling me the truth, Peter?'

'Yes, Mum.'

'Go and fetch me a coathanger!'

I heard Peter go out of the room and down the hall. The rest of us remained immobile like characters frozen in a pageant. The woman was breathing heavily through her nose. I didn't seem to be breathing at all. The child was still crying. Peter came back.

'I hope you're telling me the truth, Peter, because I'm going to thrash him within an inch of his life, and you're going to stand there and watch.'

There's a moment in an accident when you're past the point of no return. You can see everything that is going to happen, but there's nothing you can do about it. I closed my eyes and sighed. Clenched my right hand into a fist, held it in the palm of my left hand and gripped tight.

'Paul, did you tell Peter you saw me with Gerry?'

'No.'

The first shock, like diving into icy water, is always worse than what follows. I clenched my teeth and squeezed my eyes closed. I thought my arm must be broken. Then the flood banks burst. I became as numb as a jaw after a dentist's injection. I caught one glimpse of Peter. His mouth hung slightly open, and his watery blue eyes stared excitedly from his flushed pink piggy face.

I was battered slowly about the room while the woman let the hate spill out of her onto me. 'Tell me! Tell me the truth!' she howled. The coathanger broke and she threw herself in a rugby tackle which sent me sprawling on the floor. She was slapping at me, pulling my clothes and hair, scratching my arms and face with her finger nails. Exhausted, she held onto the table to haul herself to her feet, crying with frustration. 'Get up! Get up! You foul-mouthed little swine.' She picked up the broken coathanger and thrust it towards her husband. 'Claude. Are you a man? Are you just going to stand there and let him say those things. Go on!' Claude seemed to shrivel into the corner. 'Go on! Don't you love me? You can't love me if you'll let him make those accusations about your own wife and do nothing about it.' She jabbed the wood at him. He accepted it reluctantly and faced me holding it limply in his hand. 'Don't just stand there. Do you love me or don't you? Are you a man or what?' She wouldn't let him be. Too much damage had been done to her. She had too many debts to settle. She drove him with the strength of her will. His face manifested intense misery, like that of a Jew forced to marshal his own kind into the queue for the ovens. He hit at me half-heartedly.

I went to my room trying to walk normally despite the severe pain in my knee. I didn't want to give Peter the satisfaction of seeing me limp. I locked the door and examined the scratches on my forehead, cheek and arms. Bruising and swelling were beginning to show. My shirt was torn and my watch glass was shattered and the hands bent. I looked at the boy in the mirror and, despite my efforts at self-control, the cries came bubbling out.

The cries came bubbling out of Sheila as I stood before her locked in my solitary confinement. Her face was distorted into ugliness as tears ran from her eyes. 'Why are you so underhand? What's the matter with you? Why are you like this? Speak to me! Speak to me!'

Her voice chipped at me like a cold-chisel. Then she began to scream. Her looks were disfigured beyond recognition as if she had been bewitched and changed into an ancient hag. Her fists were clenched in front of her. She screamed. And screamed. I longed for her to stop. She would terrify the baby. Upset the neighbours. I moved towards her, reaching out my arms to hold her, and she recoiled as if I were reaching out to strangle her. Still screaming she ran to the table, snatched up a stool and smashed it against the floor, the table, the wall. Splinters of wood flew. Then she hurled the shattered remainder across the room. Her explosion of activity released me from my prison. Her violence pierced my stony surface like a drill and violence welled up in me and burst out like oil from a new strike. I rushed her. Grabbed her hair in my left hand and slapped her face with my right. 'Stop it! Stop it! Stop it!'

She did stop screaming, and began emitting hoarse sobs like a battered baby that hadn't strength enough to yell. She sagged, crumpled, like a rag doll, like a hunchback, like a rabid bitch, afraid, and dangerous.

I let her go and lowered my eyes to the hideous ugliness of the lino on the floor.

'Why did you hit me?' she sobbed.

'I couldn't bear watching your violence.'

'It's all right you being violent, I suppose. It's all right men being violent.'

'I'm sorry. It's not all right. I'm not saying that. You asked

139

me why I hit you. If I see violence it makes me violent, that's all I'm saying.'

It was only then that Sophie's voice penetrated my consciousness. I ran to the stairs.

'Where are you going?'

'The baby's crying.'

'What about me? What about me?'

Fuck you, I thought. I bounded upstairs two at a time. She'd obviously been yelling for some while. She'd got into a state. Her face was rage-red and wet. I picked her up, wrapped in a blanket, and walked up and down the room. 'There, there, Sophie. Daddy's here. It's all right. Did you think no one was going to come? There, there. Everything's going to be all right. Daddy's here. Daddy'll look after you.' Gradually the screaming subsided to crying, and the crying to sobbing, and the sobbing petered out. She nestled small and snug against me, and I nuzzled my face on her soft warm head and chattered soothingly as I stalked up and down the room like a caged animal.

Downstairs, I found Sheila curled up on the floor, chewing at her fingers. I went into the front room. I spread the blanket on the floor and laid Sophie on it. Sheila called out, 'I'm surprised you can find time for her – in between your fancy-women.'

The hurt and anger inside me were like dough being kneaded in a basin. There was a plastic bottle on the mantelpiece that Sheila had part-filled with rice. It had a smooth, narrow neck. I knelt beside Sophie, shaking the bottle rhythmically and humming a tune. Sophie watched intently.

Sheila came. 'Hello, my little angel,' she said. Sophie immediately turned towards her mother's voice. Sheila picked her up and petted her. That left me kneeling at Sheila's feet, the plastic bottle dangling limply from my hand. I breathed in deep and slow, struggling to hold down the urge to hit her.

'You want your mummy, don't you?' Sheila said to Sophie. 'Yes, of course you do.'

'She was all right,' I said.

'Oh. I thought you were going out.'

'You know damn well I'm not going out.'

'I thought you'd got a woman to see. You've got your coat on.'

140

She spoke quiet and calm. I yelled back, 'I've got my coat on because I haven't had the chance to take the fucking thing off yet.'

'Please don't shout when I'm holding the baby. It disturbs her.'

I jumped to my feet and jabbed a finger like a weapon towards Sheila's face. She performed an exaggerated cringe. 'Don't come your fucking school ma'am with me.'

Sophie started to cry. 'Please control your violence when I'm holding the baby,' Sheila said.

My only alternative to attacking her was to get out. I slammed the front door behind me but it hit my heel and bounced vibrating open. I turned and lashed out with my foot. The frosted glass shattered and fountained into the front room.

After being taken out of the children's home I had to start at a state primary school for the first time. It was a long walk from where I lived, through back streets, over a cinder path, along the bypass. If it was sunny I used to try to hurdle the shadows of the oncoming traffic. I could clear cars but not the long, slow-moving lorries. Wet mornings I collected cobwebs sparkling with diamonds of dew in a bent grass stem. I rarely saw other children on the way to school. I was always late.

I hated everything about school: the work; the teachers; the kids. Outside the classroom I was constantly in trouble. I used to get beaten up in the playground during breaks. Gangs would waylay me on the cinder path after school. They would twist my arm up my back, thump me with hard-knuckled fists, kick my shins with blakey'd boots, subject me to chinese burns to make me say, *I submit*. But I never would. I arrived home on countless occasions with a bloody nose.

Inside the classroom I was constantly in trouble: for being late; for being ignorant; for being insolent; for refusing to do as told; for wetting my trousers. The kids called me Pisspants. The teachers caned me. I never learnt the tables. Or the Lord's Prayer. Or the school song. My writing and spelling were appalling. I was retarded at reading. A failure at arts and crafts. A weed in PT and sports. In music, the teacher made me stand opening and closing my mouth without making a sound so that I must have looked like a child dying in a gas chamber. She said my singing sent the others out of tune.

A new boy called Billy was dumped in my class. He'd been continually shunted from school to school because he'd been placed with a series of foster parents. He was a difficult child and no one would keep him for long. The kids called him Smelly. Me and Billy shared a double desk and became friends. I was used to living with someone who was difficult, and I

142

identified with him which made me tolerant and understanding of him. I stuck up for him. Fought alongside him against the bullies who persecuted him.

I still used to wet the bed every night. It would be warm at first. Like love. Then it would go cold. I would lie awake shivering, waiting for my mother to get me up when she came to bed. She used to slap me or hit me with the hairbrush to teach me not to do it again. But I was a slow learner. She would stand over me verbally wringing her hands while I dragged the ammonia-smelling remnant of sheet off the bed. In the centre there would be a grey irregular mass, like a rain cloud. The outer edges would be dirty white like city snow. I'd use these areas to dry, first, my stomach and back and legs, and then the piece of orange rubber that protected the mattress, before putting the sodden sheet in the tin bath. Then I remade the bed. Perhaps this nocturnal exercise was the reason I always felt so tired at school.

One unbearably hot day, when children should have been outside in the sunshine instead of manacled to desks in a drab school, our teacher left the room. I rested my head on my arms and closed my eyes. As the teacher's absence lengthened, the murmur of children's voices grew louder like the drone of an approaching swarm of angry bees. The tractor outside, mowing the grass on the big kids' playing field, moaned in its ceaseless labour, the sound swelling and fading as it went up and down. Up and down. I began to sink into the soft comfort of a warm doze when I was jarred into wakefulness again. Billy was blowing on the back of my neck. Without moving I told him to stop. But he went on. And on. Anger began to boil up in me as the aggravation continued. I sat up and turned towards him. 'Stop it,' I said. 'Give over, will you?' He blew into my face like a child desperate yet unable to blow out his birthday candles. I shouted and threatened, and Billy blew.

The kids didn't like me, but they liked Smelly even less.

'Go on, Pisspants!'

'Bash him!'

The fight started in the desk. Then spilled out into the space in front of the class. We lashed out ineffectually at first but as a few wild blows landed and our anger flared we punched and kicked to hurt. Kids who sat down every morning to breakfast with proud parents around a table covered by a clean cloth, drinking from china cups with matching saucers, became a rabble ogling a Roman circus, baying for blood. '*Fight – fight – fight*!' they chanted. '*We – want – blood! We – want – blood*!'

We were torn apart by our teacher. He dragged me to his desk shouting at the class for silence. Billy stood panting and glaring with his fists clenched and his lip curled. Mr Taylor, the broken veins in his small pale face purple with indignation, brought his cane out from the desk drawer and without a word motioned me to hold out my hand. The cane swished through the hot air and burned a line across my palm. Tears came into my eyes as if I was struggling against the onslaught of a bitter wind. I held my tears back and replaced the pain in my face with a mask. I held out the other hand. Another swish. Another crack. Another scar burned into my mind. Mr Taylor nodded a dismissal. I returned to my desk with my palms pressed gently against the outside of my thighs, avoiding the gloating eyes of kids who would grow into respected pillars of society. I sat down and stared at the desk top so that I wouldn't have to watch Billy being hurt.

'Hold out your hand.'

'You ain't going to hit me.'

'Come on, boy. Hold it out.'

'You ain't hitting me.'

The crowd, drooling over the public execution they had just witnessed, held their breath with the anticipation of, even better, the spectacle of a little rebellion. The teacher, incensed that his authority was being defied, tried to get hold of Billy's **arm. Billy yanked himself free and laid into Taylor, flailing with his arms like a berserk animated windmill, and kicking out** wildly and viciously with his boots. Taylor yelped and danced back trying to hit Billy with the cane but Billy grabbed hold of it, still kicking like a crazed drunk doing the cancan. The class was on its feet. Never before had we seen the bullied little one openly fight back. My own conflict with Billy forgotten in the excitement, I shouted encouragement. 'Go on, Bill! Kick him! Kick him!'

Billy kicked and the teacher yelled. The boots cracked against his shins and knees as he retreated from the small fire-cracker of aggressive energy that pursued him across the floor.

He called loudly for help, and some of the kids (as damaged as me or Billy, but in different ways) ran forward and piled in. Still howling for help the teacher turned tail and scarpered out of the classroom. I rushed at the small police force of boys attacking the enraged frenzy that was Billy. I came behind them as they darted forward to land quick blows and then dodged back from his flailing fists and feet. Came behind them, jerking them back by their jackets, yanking them back by the neck, tripping them so they sprawled across the floor or stumbled crashing into desks. The headmaster with an army of teachers seemed suddenly to be there among us, loud mouths shouting for quiet and order, heavy hands clouting and pulling at hair, ears, clothes.

I was taken to the headmaster's room and caned on the arse six times. When I came out I passed Billy who was surrounded by a small posse of young male teachers. His face was a death mask. His eyes were burning coals of hate. 'This is your bloody fault!' he said.

I walked painfully down the verandah where, blurred by tears, I saw the diagonal shadows thrown by the roof supports across my path, like the weals across my skin, like the bars of a monstrous cage, and into the stuffy, sticky classroom with its hurting needlepricks of three dozen pairs of eyes. I eased myself carefully onto my desk seat, buried my face in my arms and cried, pestered by a plague of questions plucking at my jacket.

Billy never came back.

The sun was still shining out of a blue sky. Two mongrels had mated and were stuck end to end. A crowd of kids had gathered round them, laughing. The bigger boys were playing football and called me to join them. I hurried to the canal where I could be alone, wondering whether any of the fine slivers of flying glass could have hurt Sophie. I had fantasies of her face shredded, skin hanging in ribbons, blood streaming like tears. I tried to blot the picture out by thinking of other things, but her face kept forcing its way back, first with one cut, then many, until it was a bloodied mess – the face of a baby bearing the obscene wounds of a vicious war. I wanted to go back to them, to hold them and console them and tell them I loved them. Instead, I walked on. I continued for many miles along the canal towpath, further than I'd ever been before, seeing nothing but the dirt path, stagnant puddles, mud and dog shit.

When I finally got back I was too frightened to go into the house. Frightened Sophie would be disfigured. Frightened Sheila would be withdrawn – or venomous. I went to the fish and chip shop on the corner. It was warm, bright and friendly. There were no other customers.

'Fish and chips, please.'

'Been nice, in't it?'

'Yeah.'

'Better make most on it. Won't last.'

'Nothing good ever does.'

'Salt and vinegar?'

'Please.'

I sat on some stone steps at the side of the street to eat. When I finished I wiped my fingers on the paper, screwed it up and threw it across the pavement into the road. The cold stone was freezing my arse but I couldn't summon the energy to get up. A man and woman walked past arm in arm. They glanced my way and then turned back to their intimate chatter. Seeing their togetherness sent a pang of pain through my chest. They crossed the road and went into the pub.

After a while I got to my feet and followed slowly in their footsteps. There were very few people in the pub. The couple who'd passed me were already installed in a corner leaning across their beer towards each other, their heads almost touching. I perched on a tall stool by the bar and bought a half of Guinness. I sipped it slowly to make it last.

Every time the barmaid served or spoke to someone her face lit up in a smile. When she wasn't serving she looked as though she was about to burst into tears. She wasn't much older than me. Maybe in her early twenties. It was as though a childhood of unhappiness had marked her for life. I thought about Sophie and wondered if I would cause her so much hurt that she would be scarred too. The barmaid became aware that I was watching her. She kept looking at me and each time she caught my eye she smiled her delightful smile. And then she'd go back to her work or her thoughts and she'd look as if she was going to cry again. 'Didn't anybody love you when you were a little girl?' I asked her.

She looked taken aback. Then she smiled and said, 'I was adopted,' as if that was answer enough. And Josephine's mutilated face merged with Sophie's in my mind's eye.

I stayed till chucking-out time. When I got home I searched for blood-stains on the front-room floor, but didn't find any. Sheila had cleared up the broken glass and covered the hole with cardboard. And she'd cut out pictures from magazines and pasted them onto the cardboard to make a collage.

I sat on the floor studying the pictures. It struck me that, like myself, no one else in the street would have added that decorative touch. Social class reaches its feelers into every aspect of your personality. Class stood between me and Sheila like a sheet of glass – we could come almost as close together as two people could get, and yet there would always be an impassable barrier between us.

Eventually I went quietly up to the bedroom and got apprehensively into bed. Sheila was awake. She moved to me and wrapped her soft warmth around my coldness.

'Oh my darling,' she said, 'I thought you weren't going to come back.'

I felt as sick with guilt as an incestuous Catholic in front of the Virgin. 'Of course I was coming back,' I said. 'You know I wouldn't leave you and Sophie.'

I snuggled into her, feeling happy, and sad, and guilty, and glad to be home. Then Sophie woke. Sheila hung onto me but I wriggled out of her arms and went to the other room. Sophie stopped crying as soon as I lifted her. I carried her to the window and held the curtain back so I could see her face in the light from the street lamp. She was perfect. I started to cry then, silently, hugging her and kissing her beautiful, sleepy face. Sheila called out, 'Paul, what're you doing?'

'Coming.'

I gave Sophie to Sheila and got back into bed. Sheila tugged the neck of her nightdress down and let her full breast flop out. Sophie lay between us in the warmth, sucking sleepily. Sheila and I reached across her and held each other. She spoke to the suckling baby. 'You're a lucky little girl. You've got everything you could possibly want in the world. A mummy and daddy who love you, and love each other. And we're all together. All together.'

I listened to the breathing and gulping. The milk gurgled in Sophie's throat. I moved my head, because the pillow was wet with my tears.

It was as though Sheila and I were clinging desperately and helplessly to a wildly swinging pendulum. I remember that day she first fucked with Roger, the day I first used my belt on Sharon, the day I kicked in the glass of the front door. I remember it as the day the pendulum crazily lurched into a wider and more frantic arc.

The next day was soft and mellow, bathed in gentle colours. It was a beautiful but ordinary day in late spring. Not country spring with bluebells and cherry blossom, but town spring when the warmth radiates soothingly off the stone. The houses appeared mild and friendly, kids and dogs played in the street, neighbours lingered to chat, and people strolled leisurely. There was a hint of a smell from the bone-boiling plant – but it wasn't strong. I pushed the pram, parent-proud, to the shops, with Sheila holding the handle and pressing her cheek against my shoulder. We did the weekend shopping, made dinner, saw to the baby, sharing and touching like lovers in the first dawn of their love.

When Sophie fell asleep in the afternoon we went to bed and lay long, gently cuddling and kissing. Maybe two hours we lay together exploring each other's bodies with hands and feet and mouths. Not urgently, but easy and relaxed. And finally we fucked, Sheila lying on top of me, and me imagining I was a woman, being fucked. And then I rolled her onto her back and fucked her slow and gentle, drawing out, right out of her so that she opened her mouth thinking she'd lost me. But I kissed the wet lips of her sex with the tip of mine and sank slowly into the warm depths of her woman's body. And slow and long we moved and kissed until the throbbing beat came stronger and faster, and without my willing it my strength accumulated in my cock, and I moaned as it spurted out of me in spasms, and I tried to withdraw again but hadn't the strength, and Sheila

149

cried out as she drew me further, deeper into her, rhythmically gripping me and sucking every last drop of love juice out of me, wringing me out like a rag. And we lay on our sides, belly to belly, close and warm, my cock, still, inside her.

She spoke so softly I had to strain to hear. 'I came with you again.'

'Yeah.'

'That's wonderful, isn't it?'

'Yeah, it is. Makes me happy.'

'I never thought I would. I never thought it was possible. It never happened with anyone else.'

I felt, not hard and proud like when you've beaten someone in a fight, but soft and proud. Unthreatened. Safe and secure. Confident that I could become a perfect lover, husband, father. That at last I'd reached a place of peace. 'Everything really is going to be all right,' I said. 'I mean, if we've got that then, well, everything else will fall into place.'

'Yes.'

'It's ... I'll tell you something. Something I've never told anybody, ever. I've never even really told myself. Do you know what I mean? I've never admitted it to myself.' I took a deep breath as if I was about to plunge into cold water. I was groping for words in my mind like someone searching for a light switch in a dark strange room. 'I ... you see ... well, all my fantasies, like when I'm masturbating, or fucking somebody – you know, not making love, just fucking ... my fantasies are always about rape. I like to hurt. I like having a big cock and fucking hard so it hurts. But ... that sort of sex, when I have it like that ... it's not satisfying. Do you know what I mean? Like, I've got the urge to do it, but I don't get all that much pleasure out of it. But ... gentle ... making love, like with you, like we just did, it's ... something else. It's ... so much better.'

Sheila's voice was heavy and soft with sleepiness. I couldn't make out what she said. 'What did you say?'

'Thank you,' she said. 'For telling me that.'

It was dark when Sophie woke us, crying. I dragged my reluctant body out of the bed, and lurched across the room. To an observer from a UFO it would have looked as though I was on a boat in a rough sea. My eyes were screwed up as if I was facing into a storm. I took Sophie into our bed, but her shit smelled rotten. I got up and collected her stuff. Sheila sat up in bed and changed her and then we settled down again, but we didn't sleep. Later we got up to eat.

During the meal I felt oppressed by the wallpaper. 'They look as though they were left on someone's grave last year.'

'What do?'

'Them flowers. Let's paint the walls.'

'Oh, yes. What a good idea.'

'We'll paint them white.'

'All right.'

'Make it a bit brighter. It's like a bloody morgue in here. I'll get a load of paint and we'll do the whole room.'

'I think it might be nice white, but with maybe a coloured wallpaper just on that wall.'

'Let's just do it all white. Never mind about wallpaper. We can just slap it on all over this bloody disgusting paper. Can you imagine anybody actually *choosing* to put that on their walls?'

'We might as well do it properly.'

'Gerrout! Just slap it on.'

'If a job's worth doing ...'

'Oh, balls! We just want the place to look nice.'

'But we might as well ... '

'We're not going in for a bleeding Ideal Home competition.'

'But I want it done properly.'

I sat quiet for a while mesmerised by the miserable paper. 'Pity we haven't got some paint here. We could make a start tonight.'

'We can start to prepare it tonight.'

'What do you mean – prepare it?'

'Scrape the old paper off and get a good surface.'

'Look, love, you're not in your mum's house now. There'll be twenty bloody layers of that stuff going back for a hundred years. When you've got all the paper off, the bleeding plaster'll fall on the floor. It's only the paper that's holding the sodding walls up. Same with the lino. There'll be layer upon rotting layer of it. Pull it up and you'll fall through the floor into the sodding cellar.'

'All right. Do it your way. Only don't expect me to help.'

'Aw, come on. OK, we'll scrape it. Come on. We'll do it together. I'm sorry.'

After tea we got two kitchen knives and a bowl of water and began scraping. Sheila began in one corner and worked steadily and patiently till some hours later she'd created a small island of smooth grey plaster. I moved around, abandoning one place when it got too difficult or I'd been there too long. My wall had a profusion of patches of various patterned papers, and even one or two streaks of grey peppered with whitish holes where my knife had taken a bite and the plaster had fallen away.

It was nearly two when we went up to bed. No sooner had we wrapped ourselves around each other than Sophie began to cry. I went to fetch her. She was soaked. While Sheila changed and fed her I put dry sheets on the cot. As soon as she fell asleep Sheila tucked her in and crawled back into bed. We began kissing and fondling one another. Sheila slid down under the bedclothes and sucked me off. Then I fucked her gently until I came into her. Then kissing her, I reached down my hand and played with the lips of her cunt. It was difficult to move my arm under the weight of my body so I lay beside her. Kissing her, I fingered her gently till she seemed to be ready and then worked my fingers faster, but when she didn't come I slowed again and played more softly. I laid my head on the pillow and closed my eyes. I continued to play a medley of tunes alternately gently and then more vigorously. Suddenly she shoved my arm away and rolled onto her side. I opened my eyes and looked at the back of her head. I ran my hand over her back and buttocks and legs. 'What's the matter?' She moved away from me. I nudged up close behind and nestled around her. 'What's the matter?'

'I'm not a machine.'

'I know you're not a machine.'

'Then don't treat me like one.'

'How am I treating you like one?'

'You make me feel horrible. As though I'm disgusting. It was the same with Tom. I could tell he didn't like touching me.'

'But I'm not Tom. I do like touching you.'

'You don't. You're just forcing yourself.'

'I'm just tired, that's all.'

'But you're thinking, "I've got to keep going – to satisfy her."'

'Well, don't you want me to?'

'No. I want you to want me.'

'I do want you.'

'You just wish I'd go to sleep, don't you? I'm just a nuisance.'

'No. I'm tired, but I want it to be nice for you.'

'Big deal.'

'But for Christ's sake! You wouldn't like it if I didn't bother about you.'

'Well, if it's a bother, don't bother.'

'It's not a bother.'

'You just said it was.'

I raised myself on one elbow. 'I didn't. I just said you wouldn't like it if I didn't try to make it nice for you.'

'And I'm supposed to be grateful, am I? I'm supposed to be grateful because the *big man* allows me a bit of pleasure.'

'Well, look, some blokes wouldn't take the trouble. They'd just have their oats and roll over and go to sleep.'

She turned her face to sneer up into mine. 'Oh, and you think you're so special, don't you? You think you're God's gift to women.'

'Right, fuck you!' I pulled her over onto her back and forced her legs apart.

She struggled at first but then she lay still and snarled through gritted teeth. 'Don't do it. I'm warning you. Don't do it. I'm not going to fight you. Just don't do it, that's all.'

I realised her contempt was earned. But I was excited by her initial resistance and her surrender. I shoved into her and fucked. She lay like a body on a mortuary slab. Her mouth was clammed tight, her eyes closed and her face averted. I tried to

153

kiss her but she twisted her face angrily away. It took me a long time to come. But I kept on. Not out of sexual desire, but in order to establish some illusory mastery over her. I became a fucking machine. The sweat ran off me and collected in shallow pools on her passive body. I closed her legs together between mine so that she'd grip me tighter, so that I'd have more feeling, till at last I did come, weak and watery and without joy.

'You'll be sorry for that,' she said. I felt exhausted. I lay beside her and immediately began to slide sleepwards. She began spitting words like drops of water from a frying pan. 'You imagine ... time you were about to come ... would be like ... pulled away ... let you finish ... went to sleep ...' Like a foreign radio station that keeps fading away. I didn't answer. I just wished she'd go to sleep. Or go away. But every time I dozed she woke me, prodding me with angry words, poking me with questions. 'And where were you all that time? I'm talking to you. Who were you with?' I was being interrogated and tortured. Despite my efforts I kept losing consciousness, but each time she would shock me into wakefulness again. 'I suppose you think it's all right for you to go off whenever you're in a bad temper ... alone with the baby when I can't cope ... in no state to cope ... your fault ...'

At one point she got up, stripped the blankets off the bed and stomped out of the room. I felt guilty and wondered where she had gone. I was going to look for her to see if she was all right, to try to cuddle her and fetch her back to bed, but I fell asleep. I woke cold. I made up my mind to find something to cover myself with, but I fell asleep again. She woke me getting back into bed. I tried to cuddle up but she wouldn't let me touch her. I got warmer under the blankets and dozed off. The night tortured on towards madness. Sheila shook my arm. 'Baby's crying.'

'Wha'?'

'The baby's crying.'

'Why don't you go and get her?'

'Why don't you?'

'I always do.'

'Well, I'm too tired. I haven't slept a wink.'

The cries increased in volume and desperation. Standing up made me dizzy. I sat on the edge of the bed with my head between my legs and counted ten. I stumbled into the other room and picked Sophie up. Then Sheila started to scream. She went on and on. I walked up and down cuddling Sophie. I was cold because I was naked but I didn't want to go back to our room to get any clothes. Someone next door started banging on the wall and shouting. Sophie was upset by the screaming and thumping, and wouldn't be comforted. I was rocking her in my arms, so tired I could hardly stand. But she wouldn't stop crying. I rocked her more and more violently. Then I did a terrible thing. I started to shake her. '*Shut up! Shut up! Shut up! For fuck's sake, shut up!*'

I wasn't clear who it was I was shouting at. Sophie yelled hysterically. I looked at the wall and fantasised smashing her head against it. Smashing her against the wall till the screaming stopped. Instead I burst into tears and hugged her. 'I'm sorry. I'm sorry. I'm sorry, baby. Daddy didn't mean it. I'm sorry. It's not your fault, little Sophie. It's nobody's fault. We're just all fucked up. It's not anybody's fault.'

I carried her downstairs and dragged a stool into the kitchen so there could be two closed doors between us and Sheila's noise. I lit the oven and sat beside the stove, shivering and cradling her. The screaming subsided upstairs and gradually Sophie ceased crying too. Then the gas ran out. My money was in my jeans pocket up in the bedroom. I sat in the cold until I dozed off and nearly fell off the stool. I took Sophie upstairs. Sheila was sitting on the edge of the bed with the blankets around her shoulders. She looked like a starving Mexican whore. I placed the baby in her arms and put them into bed. I crept in beside them and we all sank into exhausted sleep.

As Sophie grew, and the spring wore on into summer, the relationship between Sheila and me got both better and worse. One day we'd be close and warm and I'd bask in more love than I'd ever experienced before. The next day she'd be shouting and screaming and the frost of her hatred would freeze up the pipes of my body so that I could hardly breathe. Each time she welcomed me into the comfort of her arms or the pleasures of her body I thought the good times had come at last, and the problems were all behind us. But as time went on she broke down more and more frequently. By the middle of summer it was nearly every day. If, when she got upset, she screamed at Sophie, she was left eating herself away with guilt, literally eating herself away, biting at her nails, gnawing at her fingers, chewing at the inside of her mouth. Then she'd force herself to be loving and giving, denying herself, until finally she couldn't keep it up any more and then she would scream at me, at the world, at the baby, and then feel guilty again. She seemed to be riding a mare as dark as night on a roundabout that was spinning dizzily, uncontrollably, ever faster.

I persuaded her to go to the doctor, but the stupid old buffer just told her to pull herself together. He gave her a prescription for a sedative. She took a spoonful mid-afternoon. She said it tasted sweet, but it didn't seem to have any effect. At teatime she took a second spoonful. By eight o'clock she was so dopey I had to carry her to bed. She slept through the night and all the following day, and only got up the next evening. She felt awful – as though she'd got a hangover; she couldn't sleep that night. She was tired and bad-tempered all the next day. Understandably she wouldn't take any more. She left the bottle in the kitchen cabinet and refused to see the doctor again.

One afternoon, after I'd had a row with Sheila, I'd walked on my own along the canal to the viaduct and was making my way back by the road. I could see a crowd of men on both sides of the main gates of the lino factory. As I got closer it became obvious there was a strike. A line of cops was trying to keep the pickets on the pavement but they were mostly spilled a yard or two into the road. There was a bit of pushing and shoving here and there like you get in a school playground, but it was all good-humoured. The blokes at the back were bawling to their mates and shouting slogans. Some of the men at the front were chatting to the coppers. I waited on the opposite pavement, watching. Behind me was a row of police reinforcements.

The atmosphere was friendly. The workers seemed glad to be out of the dark factory in the warm sunshine – pleased to be taking a stand instead of being pushed around. There was almost a carnival feeling. Then the chatter stopped. An urgent and strident voice rang out, changing the atmosphere totally like a school bell signalling that playtime was ended. 'There's one coming, boys. Don't let the bastard through.'

An intense quiet fell on the men. The police had linked arms and were trying to force the workers back onto the path. The workmen were pushing out in an attempt to block off the factory entrance. Because of the opposing pressures the line went in and out like a skipping rope if you snake it along the ground. The gigantic iron gates opened inwards. A lorry slowed to walking pace and began to turn, edging its way forward. But the space between the bulging groups of men either side of the gateway wasn't wide enough. A single voice kept ringing out. 'Don't let the bastard through!'

Unexpectedly I felt a vicious shove in my back which nearly sent me sprawling into the road. A voice said, 'Go on – piss off!'

I turned round to confront a pink young constable who

157

wasn't having much success in trying to grow a blond moustache. 'Why?' I said. 'I thought this was supposed to be a free country.' (At the times you most want it, wit deserts you and you are left only with banalities.)

'Fuck off out of it – or I'll have you for obstruction!'

I gathered up my anger and, hugging it tight, began to move slowly along the road. On the other side the swaying lines of quiet men were being edged clear of the factory entrance. A voice was raised in frustrated rage. 'Don't let these fuckers push you about!' I saw the bloke who shouted. He was middle-aged, short and thick-set, with a shiny bald head. I saw the filth facing him put the boot in his shin and then bring his knee up sharp. The man yelped twice and doubled forward, and then straightened up and punched the policeman full in the face making him stagger backwards.

There was a series of piercing whistle blasts from behind me and a few reinforcements raced across the road. A petrol lorry followed by a tight line of vehicles cut the rest off. The driver of the tanker slowed his vehicle so that he could watch the show. The filth were nipping between the traffic in ones and twos and I followed as far as the crown of the road. Half a dozen of the boys in blue dragged the bald man into the road and began punching and kicking him. One of Baldy's comrades broke out of the cordon and thumped a cop in the ear causing him to fall sprawling over a colleague's legs. He landed on his back and his helmet rolled away.

Instantly the bluebottles were all over the man like flies on bad meat. I sprinted across the road, and yelling, 'This is one for Billy!' jumped onto a cop's back. I hauled him off his prey and threw him across my leg so that he smacked onto the tarmac. At the same time I was grabbed from behind, an arm like knotted rope tightened round my neck choking me, and both my arms were twisted up my back.

As I couldn't move I went limp. My head was bent back so that all I could see was a patch of beautiful blue sky, and the flushed features of ugly pig faces. I could hear shouting and scuffling and a racing engine. I was half dragged, half carried to a navy-coloured van. The back doors were open. There was someone in there already on the floor. I was flung in on top of him like a sack of cement, so grateful to have my neck and arms

158

released that I scarcely noticed the knees and fists that helped me in. I was trying to climb off the bloke on the floor when I was flattened by two more bodies being bundled in. Then the doors slammed shut.

I asked the prone man if he was all right but he didn't answer. When my eyes got accustomed to the dark I saw his head was bleeding. One of the workmen took a handkerchief out, folded it neatly and held it against the wound. Another banged on the side of the van with his fist and shouted, 'Hey! There's an injured man in here.'

There was a lot of noise outside. I harboured the romantic hope that the workers would break through the police cordon and release us. Suddenly the van lurched forward so that we were all thrown back. Then the anchors were slammed on and we fell forward. There was a thump as though we'd hit something. The shouting outside became louder and uglier. The back doors opened and someone else was thrown in onto the injured man on the floor. The doors slammed shut and we were travelling in the dark. A voice came out of the gloom. 'What happened, Joe?'

'Bert ran in front of the van and the bastard hit him.'

'Was he hurt bad?'

'Don't know. I tried to get to him. I was slung in here.'

The men relapsed into silence. After a while I felt the need to say something – as though I had an obligation to keep up morale. 'Well, Butlin's holiday camp, here we come,' I said.

'You're right there, son. We'll be able to take it easy now.'

'You get breakfast in bed where we're going.'

'That's right. No charge for service.'

When the van stopped we sat in the dark for a while before the doors were yanked open. There were a lot of cops round the back of the van like a crowd trying to get a glimpse of a street accident. I climbed out, squinting, into the bright sunshine. It was like coming out of the pictures on a sunny afternoon. Walking caused pain to shoot through my knee and ankle.

In the police station I was photographed and fingerprinted. Then three young constables took me into another room. They shoved me about, like a handball, from one to the other, insulting me all the while. Clearly they were hoping I'd be pushed into taking a swing at one of them so they would have an

159

excuse for beating the shit out of me. I was struck by the fact that they could do me over and *say* I'd assaulted them but they were prisoners of their own authoritarianism, like a Mr Universe too muscle-bound to run or jump or throw a ball.

As I ricocheted around like a pin-ball, one of the cops said, 'What do you think you're smiling at?'

Another said, 'If you think it's so funny we'll give you a taste of your own medicine.'

It reminded me of being a child. Of being made to stand in front of my mother. Of her threats to make me smile on the other side of my face. I tried to stop smiling, but the grin spread, so I looked down at the floor. The floor was made of wooden bricks set at angles to each other like in a school. I laughed.

They decided I was a queer – too fucking chicken to stand up for myself. I was taken to another room and formally charged with the assault of a police officer at the factory gates. I said nothing at all. They asked if there was someone who would stand bail. I said no at first but they told me in that case I would have to stay in prison till I came up for trial. The only person I could think of was Roger, the pottery teacher. While they were contacting him at the college I was questioned by a sleek and civilised senior officer whose only concern seemed to be whether I was a member of any political group or organisation. He didn't realise I wasn't a worker at the factory and I didn't enlighten him. Roger must have come and signed the bail form while I was being questioned. I suppose he did it because he thought it would keep him in Sheila's good books. Their sexual liaison was still going on. I was disappointed not to have seen him. It would have been interesting to see what he was like.

It felt marvellous to be free to walk out of that frightening place into the fresh, cool, sunny evening air. I was limping, aching, tired, and I felt like singing. I looked at the sky, and breathed deeply, and despite the factory fug and the exhaust fumes, the air tasted good.

When I got home Sheila was sitting at the table with scissors and paper. She looked up angrily and then back to her work without speaking.

'Hi. What're you doing?' She didn't answer. I bent to kiss her head but as soon as I touched her she went rigid. I tried to put away the anger that filled me. It was like chucking rubbish into a cupboard and trying to hold the door against it spilling out. I slumped down on a stool by the table. 'What's that?'

'Mobile.'

'What?'

'Making a mobile.'

'What for?'

'For Sophie, to hang over her cot.'

'Great. That's nice.'

'Where have you been?'

'Got arrested.'

She looked up, trying to read my face. 'Liar.'

I shrugged.

'Did you really?' I tipped back, leaned against the wall and closed my eyes. I stretched my leg out because it hurt to bend my knee. My ankle throbbed, my jaw and ear were sore, and my kidneys ached as if I'd got flu. Sheila was unsure whether to believe me. 'What did you get arrested for?'

'There was a strike.'

'At the dole office?'

'At the lino factory.'

'What's that got to do with you?'

'Nothing. I saw the filth going at these fellers, so I tried to help.'

'That's big of you.'

'I'm knackered, Sheila. You wouldn't make me a cup of rosy, would you?'

She didn't move for maybe thirty seconds. Then she put

down the scissors and went into the kitchen. I was relishing being home. It felt like sunbathing. She brought the tea in. It was too hot to drink. She sat down and picked up the scissors but didn't start working. I was about to say, 'Your Roger bailed me out.' I was looking forward to seeing her reaction. But she spoke first. Her voice sounded unnatural. 'You're ready enough to help other people. It's a pity you can't help me.'

'I do help ...'

'You shouldn't have left me alone with Sophie all that time.'

'But I couldn't ...'

'You shouldn't. I can't cope.' She held the scissors in front of her like a murder weapon. Her hand was shaking. 'I can't cope, do you hear me?'

Her voice rose like the wail of a siren. My insides sank like a horse in quicksand. I felt stranded. I dragged my stool beside hers and put my arm round her shoulders. Her body was as rigid as if rigor mortis had already set in. 'What happened?' I tried to ease the scissors from her grasp but she snatched her hand away and clung on to them. 'Tell me. What happened?'

'I hit her.'

'What!'

'I couldn't stand her any more.' Fury exploded through my body like a charge of electricity reaching as far as my fingertips and toes. I wanted to slap her face. Instead I massaged her shoulders with my two hands. 'I can't stand her, Paul. I hate her.'

'Of course you do. All mothers hate their kids sometimes.' I thought of my mother and wondered how old I was the first time she hit me.

'Why is she so horrible? Why?'

'She's not horrible. Parents just can't cope sometimes, that's all.'

'She's hateful.'

I was trying to stay calm, but my hatred for Sheila was swelling like a malignant tumour. 'It's not her fault.'

'I hate her. I hate her. She keeps screaming all the time.'

'What else can you expect?' It was like a mousetrap snapping across the victim's vertebrae. It was out before I realised what I was saying. Sheila started to quiver. Her teeth were chattering. The scissors were shaking violently in her white-knuckled fist.

162

'You're blaming me! You think its my fault! You! You!'

'No. No. I'm not saying it's your fault. It's no one's fault.'

But she couldn't hear me. The screaming had started. A long rising note like an air-raid warning. I tried to hold her but she writhed away and shrivelled in front of me. Crouching. Shaking. Screaming. I didn't know what to do. So I sat on the stool, doing nothing.

Before the discovery of my secret woodland I'd never had the opportunity to be on my own. I'm not introspective. I'm someone who speaks and acts before I think. That is, I suppose, partly due to individual temperament, and partly because of the class I come from. The little forest became my limited university: limited, in that there were no books, no teachers; just the space and time to think. And perhaps because of the primitive and natural aspects of that environment my thoughts wandered often into the past.

Sometimes I imagined I caught glimpses of men and women from ancient times. They would move as silently as rays of sunlight among the trees, carrying a fire-hardened spear, or a stone settled in the nest of their hand. They would climb as effortlessly as orang-utans into the upper branches to scan with narrowed eyes for tell-tale movement. One would sometimes squat, stone in hammer-grip, chipping flakes from flint to form a tool with a double edge. I watched one slit the hide of a deer with a bone blade and hack the flesh with a stone axe. Babies rode piggy-back clinging onto their mother's hair or suckled at naked breasts. Children played and fought, or watched and learned.

And once I saw a group come upon a wild cherry tree. They swarmed into its branches, shaking it like an autumn squall, and within minutes had picked it as bare as winter. The mud beneath was littered with fallen fruit. They swung down and squatted, chewing, and spitting dirt. The youngsters, like starlings squabbling over crumbs, snatched quick handfuls from the earth and each other. One youth, being chased, stumbled into the stream where he dropped some of his small horde. Putting a cherry quickly into his mouth he registered pleasure and surprise. He dipped the rest into the water and washed them and ate them clean, and laughed at his discovery.

164

Some of the other young ones observed this with quizzical expressions. Then took their fruit to the water and ate and laughed and echoed his delight. That was a good day.

Walking in the drizzle along the sodden, squelching bank of the swollen stream, I would be overwhelmed with admiration for the courage and inventiveness of those long-ago people. Shaping their tools was an amazing leap forward dictated by need. But from where did the impulse come to decorate the things they made? And what passion drove them to paint those pictures on the walls of secret caves?

Their inquisitive intelligence taught them to sow seed, to domesticate animals, to trap beasts too big or fierce to fight, to construct shelters out of any materials that were to hand: hides; grass; trees; earth; ice; to make shoes and ornaments, fire and the wheel.

All that *in the face of* life. Surrounded by the competitive struggle of every other life-form to survive, this small, ill-equipped creature, not especially fast or strong, without claws, poison, armour, or even camouflage, had reached the highest pinnacle. Little children tussle to the king of the castle, young men suffer needlessly on the high slopes of Everest, in an acting out of what humankind has already achieved.

That imagination and invention created monumental works of art and astonishing feats of science. We the living were the product of all that endeavour, all that ability, all that *thrust* of body and brain.

And it had come to this.

She screamed for about twenty minutes till she was exhausted. I sat close by. Helpless. Hoping my presence was something. When the screams died away she was hunched on the floor sobbing like a baby and gulping for breath like someone who has nearly drowned. 'Paul,' she said. 'You don't think I'm going mad, do you?'

''Course not.'

I made a move towards her to comfort her, but she recoiled and her eyes widened in terror as though she could see a meat-axe in my hand so I sat down again.

'Paul?'

'What, love?'

'You won't let them take me away, will you?'

'No, love. 'Course not.'

'Don't let them lock me away. Don't let them lock me away.'

I thought, *Oh no, Jesus Christ, she's going to start off again.*

'I don't want to die inside. I don't want to die inside.' She chanted it like an incantation over and over again. 'I don't want to die inside. I don't want to die inside.' Not building up hysterically now but, disturbingly, more and more quietly as though she was turning in on herself. 'I don't want to die inside. I don't want to die inside.' Until the words became less clear as though she was drunk. I thought of things I'd heard about black masses and religious meetings where people go into a trance and strange voices talk out of their mouths. 'I don't want ... I don't ... I don't ... I don't want ... die ... die ... die ... don't ... inside ... die ... die ...' The words were slurred and then slid into incoherent noises, jabbering animal grunts. She squatted, shaking and sobbing, slobbering unintelligible sounds, like some terrible mutated toad after the next world war.

I was afraid. And revolted. And concerned. I loved her. Pitied her. Hated her. I yearned with all my being for her to

166

stop and to be like she was when things were good between us.

Eventually she subsided and was quiet. She had the face of a concentration camp survivor. I got up quietly and moved soft and slow towards her. It felt like trying to catch a bird with a broken wing that might try to fly off and batter itself against a wall or window. But she didn't panic. She allowed me to lift her and carry her upstairs. She was shivering and her teeth were chattering. I laid her in the bed, pulled her shoes off and covered her over. I climbed in beside her and held her tight until she slept. And then Sophie woke.

Sheila slept through the evening and the night and well into the next day. About midday I took her a cup of tea and some toast. She opened her eyes and looked at me but made no move to take the food or drink. 'How do you feel, love?' I asked. She closed her eyes again without answering. 'Sophie's had a bottle and some scrambled egg but she's still fretful. Do you want to give her some titty?'

'There's hardly anything there.'

'I know. But ... there's a bit of comfort in it. We all need that.'

She sighed. 'All right.'

I fetched Sophie up. Sheila still had her eyes closed. 'Do you want to sit up and have this tea?'

She didn't say anything but after a moment started to struggle into a sitting position. I held Sophie, who was crying a tearless complaining cry, on my hip. With my free hand I dragged some pillows behind Sheila's back. She took the mug, sipped, and put it down. I laid Sophie in her lap and the babe attached itself onto the nipple like a limpet onto a rock. Sheila looked down at the child with hostility. Her face was lined and her eyes were puffily swollen. Blotches on her chin and forehead glowed an angry red on her wan skin. She began to gnaw at her fingers. Her nails were bitten down to the quick and her finger ends were swollen, inflamed and bleeding. Suddenly she let out a short piercing scream and threw Sophie away from her on to the bed. Sophie howled with shock and misery.

I scooped the baby up and turned furiously on Sheila. 'What the fuck you do that for?'

'She bit me.'

'There was no need for that.'

'I'm not breastfeeding her any more. She bit me.'

'You fucking cow!'

'You feel her teeth. They're sharp. Why should I be hurt all the time?' Sheila started to cry too, like a small child. I wanted to cuddle her then but Sophie was too distraught. 'Take her away. I don't want her.'

The sympathy I was feeling for Sheila evaporated to nothing. To avoid hitting her I went downstairs. I pacified Sophie, then chucking bottle and nappies into the pram, went out. It was warm and sunny again. I walked for an hour and a half to the sea.

The girls on the promenade had suntanned legs and their breasts bounced provocatively beneath clinging summer clothes. Women in bikinis reclined on the sand. I peered at them all as I pushed the pram. I followed a girl with long hair, in a T-shirt and tight trousers, but when she stopped I couldn't pluck up the courage to chat her up for fear of being rejected. I saw a beautiful woman basking alone on the beach and thought of planting myself beside her but decided against it. Eventually I sat down by myself. Sophie started to complain as soon as the pram stopped moving.

I undressed her so that the sun could give its goodness to her body, and stripped down to my underpants. I dangled her legs in the sea for her to kick and splash. I showed her pebbles and shells and pointed out boats and sea birds. After a couple of hours she began to get grumpy. I pulled on my trousers and took her across the road to a café. They filled her bottle with warm milk. We went back to the beach and I squelched up a banana for her in my hand and gave her a rusk. I put the dress on her so she wouldn't burn and laid her down to sleep.

It was hot lying down, but cooler when you stood up because of the breeze off the sea. I couldn't decide whether to swim or not until on impulse I ran down the beach and dived into the shocking cold water. The sea washed away my troubles as if they were dirt on my skin. I dried myself on a nappy and lay on the hot pebbles beside my sleeping daughter. I felt better and stronger than I had for months. I felt that when I got home I would be able to make everything all right as I had promised.

When Sophie woke me I was cold, although it was still sunny. I packed everything in the pram and went back to the café. I had a coffee, fed Sophie an ice-cream, got her bottle refilled for the journey, and shop-lifted a bar of chocolate to take home for Sheila. Sophie was awake as we walked home so we played games. I pushed the pram ahead of me and waved bye-bye. I ran round and round the pram as we went along so that I kept appearing and disappearing from her sight. She laughed a lot. Later I gave her the bottle and trudged on slowly with my legs as heavy as tombstones. My skin prickled with heat stored up from the earlier sun.

As we neared home an old fear began to grow in me like the foetus of a deformed baby. It was a fear I'd felt every time I'd gone home to my mother's house as a child and I've carried it with me ever since. But when I turned into my street the life there warmed me once again. The fine evening had drawn the folk out of their dingy rooms onto the street. Men, after a day's imprisonment at work, sat smoking, tired, on their front steps. The women sat on chairs or cushions they'd brought out earlier in the day, or stood in tight knots here and there weaving gossip. The pigeons strutted like landlords or flew indignantly up when kids ran at them, and settled further on. Dogs chased each other or after the children playing football. Three young men peered knowledgeably into the engine of an old car. Sharon was ordering her little boy into bed. He backed slowly away from her down the road as she stood pointing at the house with one outstretched arm, shouting. When she caught sight of me she turned and walked quickly into her front room while the little lad, unexpectedly released, ran to join his friends playing in the drain outside the corner shop.

People seemed to be staring at me. Talking to one another, but staring at me. I nodded to one or two whom I knew and they nodded back politely. One of the lads from next door ran into his house and I heard him calling his mum. I put the brake of the old pram on with my foot. Aunty Doris came to her doorway. 'Paul, can you come in a minute?'

I began to feel very afraid. Perhaps Sheila had walked out on us. Perhaps she'd stuck her head in the oven. One of the little girls from over the road pulled at my shirt sleeve. 'Can I take your little lass for a walk?'

I looked down at her scraggy fair head and sad face. 'She's just fell asleep, love. Another time when she's awake.'

She turned and walked away before I'd finished speaking and joined another grubby little girl in a torn dress three sizes too big.

'What'd he say?'

'Said no.'

I went through Doris's gloomy parlour into the dim living room, as crammed with furniture as a junk shop. She'd gone on through to the back kitchen and was shouting at her boys. 'Out! Go on. Out, I said, before I clip your ears!' The back door banged and she looked in at me. 'Sit yourself down, dearie.'

'Isn't Sheila in?'

'I'm making a nice cup of tea. It's just mashing now.'

I sat wearily on a chair by the table and looked down between my legs. I noticed the seam of my jeans under the crotch had come apart and my pants, wet from swimming, showed through. I felt cold despite the heat on my skin. I wished to Christ she would just tell me what she had to say instead of making a meal of it.

In case I was in any doubt about the importance of the event she brought me the tea in her best china that normally only saw the light of day at weddings and funerals. I placed the cup and saucer carefully on the table beside me and looked into her fat old face in its frame of grey artificial curls and waited for her to speak.

'I'm afraid it's bad news, dear.'

'What is?'

'They've come and took her away.'

'Who?'

'Aye, she were in there screaming and carrying on, you know, like she does, and that old mother Hackett next door t'you, she called t'police, and they got th'ambulance, and they've took her to Littlemoor Hospital.'

I rested my elbows on my knees and pressed my palms over my eyes. I felt guilty and relieved. It was like setting down one burden and lifting up another. I remembered her pleading, 'You won't let them take me away, will you?' and I'd said, 'No.'

'If you want to leave bairn any time, we'll take care on her.' There was sympathy in her voice, and a glint of enjoyment in her old eye.

'Ta.'

'I think perhaps it was for t'best, don't you?'

'Yes. Perhaps.'

172

U p at the hospital they wouldn't let me see her. The place was huge and I didn't know which ward she was on, or even which building she was in. I'd asked a porter and he'd taken me to this hard-faced bitch who looked like a concentration camp guard.

'Are you the husband?'

'Well, yeah. Sort of. I mean, we live together.'

'Is she divorced?'

'No. Just separated.'

'Can you give me the name and address of the husband?'

'Well, that's irrelevant, isn't it?'

'Would you please give me his name and address?'

I could have kicked myself afterwards for letting myself be bullied. But I told her Tom's address and went away miserable and defeated. The following day they still refused to let me visit her so I tried to see the consultant. He wasn't there. But I saw his secretary, or maybe it was his secretary's assistant, or his secretary's assistant's secretary.

'Can I make an appointment to see him?'

'I'm sorry, Mr Greig, but Doctor Stevenson has over twelve hundred patients under his care.'

'How can he possibly look after twelve hundred patients?'

'He *is* a very busy man, Mr Greig, and you must realise that he couldn't possibly chat to the friends and relations of all his patients.'

'But ...'

'There is just no time when he could see you.'

'Well, can you tell me what's happening?'

'Yes. Mrs Hill has been committed for a period of twenty-eight days' observation. At the end of that time we will decide whether to commit her for a further period or whether she is well enough to return home.'

'When can I see her?'

'I'm afraid it's been decided, in her own interest, you understand, that visitors other than next of kin are not to be allowed.'

'What d'you mean – it's been decided? Who decided?'

'I'm afraid I can't tell you that, Mr Greig. I'm only informed of the decisions that have been made.'

'But surely, whoever's looking after her will need to speak to me to find out what's been happening to her.'

'I'm sorry. I don't know anything about that.'

'But I'm her husband.'

'I believe she has a husband elsewhere.'

'But she doesn't live with him any more. She lives with me. We've got a little girl.'

'I'm sorry, Mr Greig, there's nothing I can do.'

'But this is ridiculous.'

'I'm sorry.' Her desk and her accent were as polished as a row of bayonets. I couldn't reach across to her. She sat with a face as blank as a sheet of typing paper and her words were as empty of feeling as computer tape.

'But what about the baby? She'll want to see the baby.'

'I'm sorry, Mr Greig, I must ask you to leave now.'

'Well, what ward is she on? Just tell me that.'

'The next of kin will be informed.'

She sat like polystyrene protective packing around whatever it was I needed to get at, able to absorb all the knocks and bumps. I didn't even want to hit her – not because it would have been futile but because I felt defeated. I went home to Sophie.

The next day I went up to the hospital at visiting time and wandered around peering in windows like a peeping tom hoping to catch a glimpse of Sheila. That evening I found Sheila's address book and went out to the phone box to ring her mother. I told her Sheila had sent a message requesting some of her things. The old tart was tart, but told me the ward number. I went there at visiting time the following day and discovered it was a locked ward. I hovered around but failed to find a way to get in. The next day I shaved and made myself look as respectable as I could. I went to the reception desk and presented myself as Mr Hill. A porter took me to the ward and knocked on the door. I heard a key turn on the inside. The door

174

opened and a nurse showed me in. It was a huge room with twenty or thirty beds at one end, seats and tables at the other, and an office in the middle. The nurse pointed to Sheila who was sitting on a settee in a dirty-white hospital-issue nightdress and a drab dressing-gown, doing nothing. I went across and sat beside her. She appeared to be gazing at the artificial flowers in a bowl on the low table in front of her. I spoke quietly, frightened of doing or saying the wrong thing.

'Hello, love. How are you?'

She turned her face to look at me. She was so pale she looked as if she had been drained of blood – like my mother used to look when she was brought back from hospital in the early hours. Her eyes were glazed and when she didn't move or speak I thought she didn't recognise me. But then her mouth slowly puckered up like a baby's and her bottom lip quivered and the tears started to spill out of her eyes. I wanted to hold her like I held Sophie and save her from all the hurt in the world. I put my arms round her and held her wet face against mine and bit into my lip to stop from crying.

Her body shook gently like an idling motor. Her voice was the voice of a little child. 'Why didn't you come before?'

'They wouldn't let me. The bastards wouldn't tell me where you were. I had to pretend I was Tom to get in.'

'How's Sophie?'

'She's fine. How are you?'

'I'm so glad you've come.'

'How has it been?'

'It's been terrible.' She was talking between sharp intakes of breath and sniffs. Her breath smelt bad.

'Has your mum been? Or Tom?'

'Nobody.'

'What's been happening to you?'

'I wish you hadn't gone out and left me.' The tears began flowing faster.

I looked away from her. A sunken-cheeked ashen-skinned old lady was staring at me with her mouth hanging open, a dribble of spittle down to her chin. I looked at the flowers in the imitation glass bowl. 'I'm sorry.'

'Wish you hadn't. I was so lonely. So lonely. That's why I was screaming. I wanted someone to come. To take care of me.

175

It was all right when they came. But they brought me here. I'd stopped crying then. I felt better. But they tried to make me take these pills. To make me feel better. But I did feel better already. They said they would quieten me down. But I was quiet already. I wouldn't take the pills. They said they were keeping me here for observation. I said I felt all right and anyway how could they observe me if I was doped up. I said all they would observe would be the effects of the drugs. I wouldn't take them so they held me down and injected me with a needle. I screamed and fought. But there were too many of them. They were too strong. They were male nurses and they enjoyed it. They were holding me down by my breasts. They were laughing. They injected me and I passed out and woke up in a cell. I was all on my own, Paul. And whenever I screamed because I didn't want to be on my own they came back and injected me again and put me to sleep.'

I was in turmoil. The guilt, the pity, the rage, were manufacturing and releasing chemicals in my body that were working at odds with each other. My feelings were so intense and so contradictory that I felt blown apart. I felt shell-shocked. 'Bastards. Fucking bastards!'

'I didn't want to take the pills.'

'That's right, my love. Don't take them.'

'But I do now, Paul. I have to. They kept me locked up on my own for punishment. I couldn't stand it. I do now. It's better here because there's other people. It's better than being on your own, Paul.'

'Jesus fucking Christ, we've got to get you out of this hellhole. Come. Now. Come with me now.'

'I can't. They've taken my clothes away.' She sounded totally defeated. She spoke unbearably slowly, slurring her words.

'Where are they?'

'I don't know.'

'Listen. I'll come tomorrow. I'll bring a case with your clothes. No – not a case. I'll bring a carrier bag. You can go in the bog. Yeah? Get changed. Then we'll walk out like two visitors. If they see us we'll run for it. Fuck! I wish we had a bleeding car. I want to get you as far away from this place as possible. All right now? Tomorrow we'll get you out of here. OK?'

The next day I went to the porter's lodge anxiously clutching a Co-op carrier bag. I said I was Mr Hill. The porter looked surprised and then his eyes narrowed in suspicion. 'Then who were that I just took in?'

'I don't know.'

'He said he were Mr Hill. Said he just come in t'train from down south to see wife.'

I stood staring like a dummy, not knowing what to say, fighting back tears of helplessness and frustration. I turned and ran out of the doors and down the drive and only slowed to a walk when I got to the gates, and then only because I was afraid someone might mistake me for an inmate escaping.

I didn't dare show my face at the porter's lodge again, but every afternoon I left Sophie with someone on the street and went up to the hospital to hang around outside the ward watching for a chance to nip in. About a week after Tom's visit I came upon a trolley round the back of the ward at the bottom of the fire escape. A porter was carrying cardboard cartons up the iron stairs. As soon as he disappeared into the ward I followed him up. The door stood slightly ajar so I walked in. Nobody noticed me. I could see the porter through the office window talking to a nurse. He looked like a Christmas shopper with his arms full of parcels. Most of the patients were up the day end of the room, but Sheila was sitting on the side of a bed not far from me. Her lined face was as white as the belly of a dead trout. There were puffy blue bags under her eyes and her eyelids were pink and swollen. She'd aged twenty years in two weeks. She stared vacantly into space like a blind person. I went to her and sat very carefully on the bed beside her fearing her fragility, afraid she might break as easily as a thin-shelled egg clutched in a child's hand.

'Sheila.'

She looked at me but gave no sign of recognition. She had a handkerchief in her nail-bitten bleedy hands which she wrenched and twisted this way and that as though it were a tiny animal she was trying to strangle. She was chewing at the inside of her cheek.

'Sheila, I've brought your things.' I offered her the carrier bag. She made no move to accept it, staring at me as if I were a stranger or an enemy, all the time torturing the animal in her hands and biting her own flesh. 'Sheila, come on.'

I put my hand on her shoulder but she gave no indication that she knew I was touching her, as though she was totally numb. She shook her head from side to side as slowly and sadly as a caged elephant. Her words were slurred. 'Sno goo'.'

'Come on, Sheila. We've got to get you out of here. The fire escape's open over there. Get dressed quick and we won't have to trick the nurses into opening the door.' She just went on shaking her head. 'What's the matter, Sheila – are they doping you up?' Her head-shake changed into a slow nod. 'You mustn't let them. You mustn't take that stuff.'

'Got to. Make you.'

'Sheila. Are you coming?'

She went back to shaking her head. All the anger that I'd known in her face for so long was gone. She was broken. And her words broke me. 'Got to be a goo' girl.'

I glanced hopelessly round the ward. There was a nurse down the far end talking angrily at an old lady as if the old lady were a child. The scene reminded me of Miss Batt threatening one of the little ones in the children's home. The old one was an island in a pool of piss and her head hung in shame. She nodded at everything the nurse said. I could see the other nurse through the open office door signing a sheet of paper for the porter.

'Sheila, I'll have to go.'

She bowed her head, screwing the handkerchief as if trying to wring blood out of it, chewing her cheek as if intent upon gnawing a hole through her face. The porter was walking back towards the fire exit. It was clear Sheila wouldn't come. Couldn't come. And I believe she'll never walk out of that place. Looking down the corridor of years ahead of her I can only see an old lady with wet drawers nodding in shame and repeating, 'Got to be a good girl. Got to be a good girl.' I bent and gently kissed her twisted moving mouth. She didn't respond or recoil and her lips were lifeless. It was like kissing a loved one's corpse the last time before the coffin lid is screwed down. I hurried across to the door as the porter was about to close it. 'Just been visiting my wife. Might as well come out this way. It's quicker.'

'OK, mate.'

He forced the key into the lock. I glanced back at Sheila, still sitting on the bed, murdering the handkerchief and biting the inside of her mouth, staring into the emptiness of her future. If she'd looked at me I would have had to go back. But she didn't. I pushed past the porter as I started to cry. Hoarse stifled sounds escaped from my throat and tears blurred my vision so that I stumbled on the stairs as I heard him bang the door behind me and twist the key.

I didn't go back to the hospital. I took care of Sophie as best I could but she grew increasingly fretful. New teeth coming through, a cold she couldn't shake off – really she just wanted her mum. It didn't seem much to ask, yet we were crying for the moon.

After the twenty-eight-day period I phoned Sheila's mother. They'd recommitted her. Indefinitely. 'They must be crazy,' I said. 'They're bloody insane.'

'They said she's a very ill girl.'

'She needs to be loved, to be taken care of – not shut away.'

A lorry rumbled past outside the phone box drowning her words.

'What?' I said.

'I said it's a pity you didn't think of that earlier before you broke up a happy marriage.'

'What the fuck are you on about? Don't talk crap to me. You were her mother. Who do you think did the damage? She was fucked up years before I ever met her. I was the one left trying to pick up the pieces of the mess you created. Where was the love you should have given her? Your fucking dugs must have dried up before you even fed her.' She was yelling at me but I couldn't hear what she was saying because I was yelling back. 'Don't you try to turn everything away from yourself. Don't try to make me the scapegoat for your fucking failure!'

But she'd slammed the phone down. I stood with the receiver in my clenched fist and looked through the glass at the pram outside. I couldn't see Sophie. She was sleeping. But I spoke quietly to her anyway. 'It's not her fault, Sophie. Poor old cow. She was just passing the damage on down the generations, like pass the fucking parcel. Oh, Sophie. Where will it end?'

I laid the receiver gently in its cradle. Then I span round and lashed out with my foot and the glass smashed and shattered across the pavement. The faces of passers-by were turned towards me by the sound. 'Fucking phone box vandals,' I screamed at them. 'What else can you fucking expect!'

It was one of those days when the sky is covered with a patchwork of white on blue and yet cloud hardly ever obscures the sun. I sat with my back against the secure strength of a tree many years older than me. I felt both calm and acutely aware. I fancied I could almost hear the throb of life that surrounded me, almost feel the pulse of nature.

And as I sat there in the little wood, I tried to make sense of life. I'm ignorant. I know little, and understand less. My knowledge is an accumulation of half-digested scraps that have fallen from other people's feasts.

I knew that life on earth was nothing but an accident of gas and circumstance. For thousands of millions of years we were bacteria in a warm sea that stank of rotten eggs. Until we discovered sexuality. Sexuality provided genetic variation. It was like the difference between the slow, laborious and detailed preparations on the ground, and the phallic thrust of a rocket taking off. We became a soft and shapeless mass on the ocean floor and then a floating jelly, and already we'd developed the ability to hurt. We burrowed for safety into sand, and created armour to protect our back. With backbone and jaws and new-found mobility we became masters of our element – before we abandoned it for another. We dragged ourselves onto land and discovered our voice. We became nimble enough to scurry across the carpet laid down by ancient forests and clamber into the protective arms of trees. We tried our sharp teeth on insects, fruit and leaves. With grasping hands we swung beneath the branches. With forward-facing eyes we leapt gracefully from tree to tree. And when the branches broke under our increasing weight we fell back to earth, like seed when the time was ripe. We lived in groups, sharing skills and knowledge, and learned the language of co-operation. We began to use sticks and stones as

182

tools and weapons. We came out of the forest and stood upright, alert to threat. And learned to hunt.

All the seemingly infinite variety of life was the product of sexuality: the drive to reproduce; the genetic variation; the flourishing of those most suited for the struggle to survive. We had to strive to learn new skills at every juncture on the way. A tiny shrew strove to climb with fierce courage and commitment. *He* was the one who increased his food supply, who was safe from the dangers of the forest floor, who fucked the female, who passed on his genes. He was the father of us all.

The males of his line fought for mates, were driven by irresistible instinct into females. The agile, with their physical prowess, the cunning, with their larger brain, the fortunate through favourable mutation, are in our blood. I felt the surge of their impulse in me. I felt that instinct to fight for a female, that urge to plant my seed.

And yet. Where would that lead? Where had that led? I yearned for a woman on heat to come through the wood to the bank of my stream. But what future would there be – for her? For our progeny? For me? What use was nature in a world of artificiality?

Throughout the summer I went on seeing Sharon every week. I usually slapped her or carefully belted her or tore her clothes before I fucked her. It was like some strange religious ritual. I used to make her get on her knees to suck me off. Once, wanting to find some new way of hurting, I buggered her. It gave me pleasure to see her cry.

I realised that I hated her. That I hated women. That I hated myself. There was nothing decent in my life except the little love I had for my baby.

Sophie used to wake every night. I'd get up, change her, make her a bottle, and take her into the warmth of my bed. (But it was never as warm as it had been with three of us.) I'd feed her and cuddle her and tell her I loved her, and that her mummy loved her, and that if Sheila could see us snug and warm in her bed it would make her happy.

One Thursday I met Sharon in heavy rain. She was sheltering under a tree and her hair was dark and damp and her face shiny wet. I'd never seen her look so lovely.

'I don't want to do it today, Paul,' she said.

'Don't you?'

'No. Don't make me.'

I grabbed a handful of her hair and hauled her through the sodden wood. I stripped her and laid her naked on a bed of wet earth, rich-smelling and soft with leaf mould. I *looked* at her for the first time. Her body was small-boned, firm, smooth-skinned, and shapely, but her hands and feet revolted me. Her hands and feet were repulsive, big and red and shapeless like slabs of raw meat. I fantasised slicing them off her with a butcher's cleaver so that the stumps spouted blood like crimson springs. I wanted to be able to cleave the ugliness from her.

I strapped her harder than I'd ever done before, and then pinning her arms to the ground, with her legs over my shoulders, I fucked her, penetrating so deep that each of my thrusts was answered by a cry. It was all over quickly. Too quickly. Then she dressed and we started to walk homewards, slipping and sliding on the wet earth. The rain dripped off my hair and trickled down my neck. Sharon took hold of my arm. Her hands were surprisingly warm and soft.

'Paul?'

'Yeah.'

'I'm not coming any more.'

I didn't say anything for a while, watching for brambles and nettles and fallen wood. 'I'm not surprised.'

'It's not that. I like what we do. But Dick knows there's some'at going on. He says if I'm fooling around with anyone he'll kill 'em.'

'Kill me? Well – why not?'

'And he'll kill me too.'

I stopped walking, and she turned back to look up at me. 'It's ta ta, then,' I said.

'I'm not coming any more, Paul.'

'OK.'

'Is that all right?'

'Sure. Ta ta.'

'Bye.' She looked surprised and upset. I suppose, if as a child, you have only ever been cuddled after being hit, craving love, you seek hurt. What else could you expect? Her father had thought kids were women's work. Her mother, receiving none, never had affection to give: only guilt after beatings thawed her inhibitions. Sharon, the mother, still the hurting child, turned and started to walk away down the hill towards the canal.

'Sharon!' She stopped and turned back. 'Wait a minute.' I went to her, ran my hands down her wet hair and held her head. I kissed her a lingering gentle kiss in the rain. 'Sharon,' I said. 'Love your little ones. Whatever they do. Love them, Sharon. It's their only chance.'

''Course I love them.'

'No. I don't mean that. I mean something more than that.' She didn't move. Just held on to me as if she would go on standing there all day. I stepped back. '*Bye bye love,*' I said. '*Bye bye happiness. Bye bye sweet caress, I think I'm gonna die.*' From the sublime to the ridiculous.

She looked puzzled. 'Bye bye, Paul.'
'And thank you,' I said.
'What d'you mean?'
'Just thank you.'

I haven't fucked a woman since. Except inside my mind. Raping and thrashing inside my head where I don't need to hold back but can lash out with all the uninhibited frenzy my mother unleashed on me.

In my fantasy the woman I rape is always ambivalent. She resists but is excited. And finally she surrenders totally. And then I am the woman – being raped by me. And I say, 'It doesn't matter how much you hurt me, Paul. I still love you. Whatever you do – I'll still love you.'

I identify with children, with victims, with the underdog, with the weak against the powerful. I don't want power. Except over women. Except in sex. But then I become the enemy. Rape is a crime of the powerful against the weak. I want to rape the woman I love. I want to do this worst of all possible things to her to test her love. I want her to say, 'It doesn't matter what you do. I will still love you.'

That's what children need their parents to say. Not in words. But in living. In giving – not things, but time, attention, comfort, warmth.

I gave what warmth I had to Sophie. Now I am cold.

The last time I visited my retreat was on a day of dazzling heat. But in the wood it was cool and damp. Goosegrass, hogweed, bracken, bramble, and fern formed a green chest-high thicket as they jostled each other for light. My nostrils were filled with the scent of summer woodland, must and garlic and honeysuckle. The varied drone of insects accompanied the twitter of birds, and the ceaseless gushing of the stream was counterpointed by the rustle of summer's leaves. I fought my way down to the bank of the stream and squatted on a rock to splash tingling water into my sweaty face. Red-and-black and white butterflies chased each other into the undergrowth. A bee hovered like a gourmet spoiled for choice above a hogweed's dish of flowers. A dazzling dragonfly, the vivid blue-green of a drake's neck feathers in spring, darted hither and thither above the surface of the stream. It was hardly believable that this lush and verdant jungle was the same barren winter woodland I had first found back in February. I sat on the moist earth with my back against a tree and turned my face up to the fragmented sun. The high foliage moved incessantly with the languid rhythm of a boat moored on a calm sea. I closed my eyes and gazed at the red kaleidoscopic pattern under my lids, allowing my mind to be overwhelmed by the extravagant profusion and variety of all the forms of life that had grown from that chance meeting of gas and electricity when the earth was naked and new.

I let my mind wander back into prehistory and beyond. I thought about our universe – and beyond that. Our planet had been thrown up by the sun. But where had the sun come from? Perhaps all the stars in all the universes had been scattered, like seed from the hand of a peasant, by the explosion of one original gigantic mass of fiery rock. But where did that come from? What came before that? What would come after? What could be the frame within which we existed? Outside our universe, there were other universes. Outside them, what? More still? And surrounding them all? Space? And surrounding space? Somewhere there must be an end? A beginning? In nothing? I found myself spinning in a black hole. Panic possessed me. Sweat, caused not by heat, but fear, turned into trickles of terror burning my skin, collecting in pools of dread.

I opened my eyes, labouring for breath. I had palpitations in my chest as though a panic-stricken bird was trapped in the cage of my ribs. I shivered with cold beneath a coating of perspiration. I needed someone to hold. I was going mad. I was frightened of going mad.

Sophie and I stayed at home, only leaving the house to go to the dole or the shops. I became increasingly paranoid. Scared Dick would round up some mates. Scared Tom would hire some hard men. Whenever I had to open the door I expected to find a man with a machine gun on the other side. Every time I came downstairs I held my breath expecting to hear shots and feel lead ripping through my guts. On the street, footsteps behind frightened me into looking round to see if I was being followed. A car approaching, if I was crossing the road, made me run for a corner or doorway or lamp-post in case it mounted the pavement to run me down. If a car stopped ahead of me I expected to see the doors fly open and armed men spill out.

I only went out if I had to. I didn't go to the court on the day I was summoned. I've been expecting the police every day since. Whenever I saw the filth on the street I fantasised pulling a gun and pumping bullets into the soft belly of the bastard, seeing his face surprised and scared and distorted and ugly, and seeing him fall at my feet with the warm blood spilling out of him flowing slowly and thickly like lava across the pavement into the gutter. My fantasies turn the tables on my fears and nightmares. Night after night I dream of being hunted, imprisoned, killed.

The last time I went out was to collect my dole. I arrived ten minutes earlier than my signing-on time. The clerk made me stand ten minutes at the counter before he'd let me sign, and then told me my money had been stopped. When I asked why he shrugged. I looked at his chubby complacent clean-shaven face and I wanted to thump it into pap. But I kept reminding myself I already had one assault charge coming up, and they'd never give me bail a second time. Who would take care of Sophie then?

I went to the claims office and sat for two hours in a steaming and smoky room that smelled of stale cigarettes and dampness from rain-wet clothes. Sophie sat on my lap. I played with her for a while and then she cried for about an hour before falling asleep. When they called my name I carried her through to the booth.

'Mr Greig?'

'Yeah.'

'Sit down.'

'Why have you stopped my money?'

'You've been unemployed for well over a year now, Mr Greig. We can't go on paying you indefinitely.'

'But I'm signed on at the labour exchange.'

'Yes, but you have to help yourself too. You can't expect others to do it all for you.'

'I haven't refused any jobs. If they haven't sent me after any it's because there aren't any about.'

He was a middle-aged man, dressed as if he were going to a funeral straight from work: dark suit, stiff collar, black tie. He had a bald head and round glasses in gold frames, and the sort of prim little mouth you might expect to find on an elderly spinster school-ma'am or one of Hitler's aides. He sat on the other side of the counter pressing the top of his fountain pen against his lips, looking down at the wad of papers, held together on a card by a thick elastic band, that he took to be me. 'Mm. Can you tell me, Mr Greig, what efforts you are making to find yourself employment?'

The bastard wouldn't look at me. Sophie cried out in her sleep and raised one shaking clenched fist like a communist salute. 'I can't look for work at the moment.'

'Oh. And why not?'

'I've got this baby to look after.'

'And what about your ... your cohabitee?'

'She's ... had a breakdown. She's in hospital.'

He shuffled quickly through the papers. 'You don't appear to have informed us about that.'

'No.'

'You know that you are obliged to inform us of any change of circumstances.'

'I ... I didn't think about it.'

'How long ago did she ... go into hospital?'

'Don't know. Couple of months.'

'This is very serious. Do you mean to say that you've been making a false claim for "a couple of months"? You realise that this is an offence in law. You've been obtaining money from the state fraudulently.'

'I don't know about that.'

'Well, I'm telling you about it. You'll be hearing more from us about this. In the meantime your money will be stopped.'

'How the hell are we supposed to live?'

'You'll have to work, Mr Greig, like the rest of us.'

'But there is no bloody work. And anyway I've got this child to look after.'

'You'll have to put it in a nursery. Or find someone to look after it during the day. It's hardly a man's work, in any case.'

'Don't call my daughter an "it". She's not a thing. She's a human being. And I'm her father. And I'm not going to put her away every day. I'm not going to leave my child to be fucked up by someone who's doing it because they need the money or because ... '

'Kindly keep your voice down, Mr Greig, and remember where you are. If you are sincere about wanting to support your child I'm sure you will leave no stone unturned to find yourself employment.'

'What d'you mean, find myself employment? I'm already fully employed looking after my daughter. How can I take care of her if I'm not bloody well there?'

'I have asked you to lower your voice. If you don't feel that you are able to support the child and to take care of her adequately I suggest you find another home for her. You could have her adopted or fostered ... '

'Do you know what you're saying?' I was on my feet talking quietly now in a shaking voice. I felt as cold as if I were inside a deep freeze. My mouth was dry and my skin taut pulling my face into what felt like a grimace or snarl. 'Have you ever been in a foster home? Have you? Well, I bloody have.' Sophie was still sleeping crooked in my left arm as I leaned across the counter jabbing my forefinger like a bayonet towards the man's face. He slid his chair backwards to stay out of my reach. My voice rose with animal fury. 'So don't speak to me about fucking foster homes because I fucking well know.'

192

He hovered by the door attempting to appear composed, but pale and trembling. 'If you can't cope with your duties as a parent, Mr Greig, then the child will have to be taken into care.'

'*Taken*!' It was more of a howl than a spoken word. Sophie woke with a start and began screaming. I pressed against the counter with my thighs trying to walk through it, reaching out my hand for the throat of that man I wanted to kill who hastened away out of sight through a door which closed behind him. '*Taken! You'll take my child away from me over my dead body! I'll fucking murder her first! Do you hear!*'

I'd decided not to open the door to anyone. I'd spent the last of the money at the corner shop. By Sunday there was no food left – nothing but the two pints of milk the milkman delivers each morning. Sophie cried nearly all the time she was awake. I just sat with her while she cried. Sat like a dead man and watched her cry. And in her crying I heard the pain that I'd suffered and the pain that I'd caused. I sat helpless. There was nothing I could do.

She had a sleep on Friday afternoon. It was a week of Indian summer. It was stuffy inside the house. Like the inside of a coffin. I took a chair out into the back yard but the sickly smell from the bone-boiling plant above the town was so strong I had to come in again. I sat staring out at the sun-scorched yard through the window, closed against the smell.

I imagined a room of colossal vats like vast witches' cauldrons; and pigs being dragged squealing up to the vats and being butchered; and butchers in blood-splattered aprons, their boots slap slap slapping in the blood as they moved at their work, slicing open the warm bodies so that blood spurted in fountains and gushed in rivers across the floor. The butchers were tugging guts from the steaming bodies with big blood-stained hands, like brutal midwives tearing babies from womb-warmth to an early death. And, watching, I became gradually aware that the animals being hauled squealing across the floor to the butchers were not pigs – but people. Men and women and children. Dragged by the arm or leg by others stronger than themselves. There were parents there carting in their own children. Handing their own babies over to the butchers who dismembered their beautiful bodies, hacked the meat from their bones, and hurled the bones into the huge vats of boiling fat.

Suddenly I realised that Sophie was crying upstairs. I sat for a moment trying to pull myself together. I didn't hear the slap Doris next door gave her son, but I heard the boy cry out and I flinched. I felt myself shrivel into a little boy with an old man's face standing in front of a suffering mother who had no love to give.

*

I sat on a chair in the gloom-filled living room with the baby on my lap, holding the bottle to her mouth. She drank greedily and the level of the milk fell rapidly. I sang a lullaby to her, making up the words as I went along.

Hush, little Sophie, don't you cry, I'd like to give you the summer sky,
and if that sky turned sunset red, I'd like to give you a piece of bread,
and if that piece of bread went stale, I'd like to give you a drink of ale,
and if that drink of ale went flat, I'd like to give you a pussy cat,
and if that pussy cat should go, I'd like to give you the winter snow,
and if the winter snow should thaw, I'd like to show you a secret door,
and if that secret door should close, I'd like to give you a red, red rose,
but you know that red, red rose would die,
so hush, little Sophie, don't you cry,
Daddy's gonna love you till you die.

I sang it over and over and it became a monotonous dirge. Her eyes that had been looking up trustingly into mine began to close, as though the lids had become too heavy, though she fought to stay awake – like a wounded salmon struggling against a stream that has become too strong. Her eyes rolled under half-closed lids and her sucking ceased. I turned the bottle up. There was about half an inch of greyish milk in the bottom. I put the bottle on the floor beside the chair. Sophie's eyes closed but her mouth began making weak sucking movements. I carried her into the kitchen and put some of the syrup in a teaspoon and tipped it into her mouth. She took some and coughed, and a dribble of grey ran down her face and under her chin. I wiped her face with the teacloth, then went back to the chair in the other room and sat with Sophie on my lap in the dark, looking down at her but hardly able to see her. Except in

196

my mind's eye.

She wasn't beautiful. Not like her mother. More like me, I suppose. She was *my* baby. She lay very still. 'Sophie, baby, I'm sorry,' I said. 'So sorry. I wish you could understand. I'm not doing this to hurt you, but because I love you, because I want to save you from being hurt. For twenty-one years I've been a mouse in the claws of the world's cat. I want to save you from that torment. I don't know where the world went wrong, Sophie, but it got in a muddle and no one can seem to sort it out. I wanted to find some way to teach you to fight, without wanting to hurt. Because I want to hurt and I'm frightened to fight. I just keep hurting people. People keep hurting each other. It's a cycle, Sophie, with no beginning and no end. When we're little we're hurt by our parents because of the damage done to *them*. We're never given enough love, so when we grow up and try to live with someone we drag along with us this outsize need: a need to be loved like a little child should be loved. But that's too big a demand – it's an impossible need for anyone to satisfy. That other person has been hurt too. That other person was never loved enough. You're each demanding too much from the other. You're both crying out to have all those years of emptiness filled. It's like saying: People have been scooping out stone from this quarry for hundreds of years – I want *you* to put it all back! If neither of you has been loved enough, how can you have love to give? If nobody's pouring any in, you don't have any to pour out. You run dry. If people keep pouring in hurt, that's what you're full of – that's what spills out. And each time you're hurt the accumulated pain of all the other times you've been hurt, right back to babyhood, overwhelms you and in your agony you lash out and hurt whoever is within reach. And who's within reach? The people closest to you. The person you live with. Your own children. And your children grow up and have babies of their own and do the same to them. And it goes on and on and on. Oh God, oh God, oh God, oh Jesus fucking Christ, Sophie, when will it ever end?'

The day Sophie was released from pain was a good day. She'd learned to crawl. She'd laughed a lot. She'd gone to sleep soothed by the sound of a lullaby. Her last experience was of being cradled in her father's arms – of being loved.

I held the cushion over her face for a long, long time. There was no struggle. I sat for an hour in the black room talking to the cold baby in my arms. Then I carried her upstairs to her room. She was stiff. I switched the light on. Her eyes were closed but her mouth was open and swollen. Her skin was white. Not yellowish-white like paper – more like white stretched over blue like porcelain. Her lips were mauve and her tongue swollen and black. Her fingers and toes were a delicate eggshell blue. I wrapped her in blankets and laid her in the cot. I bent over and kissed her forehead. Then I switched off the light, came out and closed the door.

I sat down at the table and began writing on the back of the wallpaper we'd bought and never used. I thought it would be just a short note about what I had done. About what I was going to do. But then I wanted to understand. I want you to understand. I wrote through the night. My finger became so sore from holding the pen that I had to put a plaster on it. I wrote all the next day. I've been writing for three days now. I haven't been back to the room. I haven't looked at her again. I want to remember how lovely she was – how full of life. I've had no food. Just the two pints of milk the milkman leaves every day. I'm afraid I'll have to leave him a bad debt.

The second night I slept. I dreamed of Sophie all night. Of Sophie and Sheila. Of babies being butchered. The weather hasn't changed and the smell from the bone-boiling factory was seeping into my bedroom. I couldn't smell Sheila any more in my bed. Only the stench of boiling bones.

I had another dream in which I was a member of a small guerrilla group. We were being squeezed by a military force that was encircling us. We withdrew into the park. There were only four of us left alive. A couple were wounded. In the park was an air-raid shelter left from the last war. We groped our way down into the inhospitable dark with its rank stink of piss and damp. We were as blind as moles until our eyes became accustomed to the gloom. We knew the army had surrounded us, was closing in, that there was no hope. But we cocked our guns and waited and smiled silently to each other. And then we heard boots on the concrete steps, and two soldiers with machine guns burst in and started firing randomly into the shadows. One fell. And so did my comrades. I was hit. I tried to fire but had no ammunition left. I found a knife in my hand. I ran and threw myself at the enemy so that he fell on his back on the dank stone floor. I was above him and I leaned down with all my weight pressing the knife into his abdomen. As I felt my weapon sink into him he half closed his eyes and opened wide his mouth like a woman in orgasm, and there was a thread of spittle across his lips. And then we lay still, and I realised with shock that the soldier was a woman. We looked into each other's eyes without hatred or malice and I saw the life draining out of her as I felt it draining out of myself, and the boots clattering down the steps behind me didn't matter for I realised that we two had become one. And I was at peace.

And last night I dreamed I was in a city. A mass meeting in the streets. And then the troops came. There was panic. The crowd scattered and I scampered through side streets and alleyways until I came onto a large deserted square. There I found that every exit was blocked. Tanks came rumbling, crunching over debris and the limbs of the fallen, bursting through barricades; and the ground trembled. I backed into a space between a stone wall and a telephone kiosk – a place of concealment only wide enough for a hunted beast. I saw the tanks come rolling, slowly, relentlessly, round the square, marking out their territory, their engines roaring with inhuman power. The foremost tank drew abreast of my retreat. I ached for it to pass me by, but though its motor growled on, it stopped in its tracks, and the big gun that had pointed the way forward swung in a slow arc and came to rest aimed at me. I crouched and shrivelled into myself, like a speeded-up film of a foetus unfolding in the womb shown in reverse. I could see nothing human. Only the mass and might and inhumanity of the heavily armoured machine. The only direction I could move was towards the muzzle of the gun – a dark tunnel of pain leading to an infinity of nothingness. There was no other way. I knew the end had come.

FIVE FOR SORROW TEN FOR JOY

Rumer Godden

It's the year of liberation in Paris when English born Elizabeth
meets the hypnotic, seductive and sadistic Patrice. And so
begins her tragic journey through love, prostitution, murder
and imprisonment to the serene tranquillity of the convent.
But even the Sisters of Bethanie cannot help her avoid forever
a shattering confrontation with her past, her future and her
faith.

'Miss Godden knows how to tell a story and yet again will
give pleasure to her many devoted admirers.'
SUNDAY TELEGRAPH

'A very readable and dramatic story of manipulation, violence,
double dealing and redemption.'
FINANCIAL TIMES

'A first class story with a rich and unusual plot.'
EVENING STANDARD

Futura Publications
Fiction
ISBN 0 7088 1842 0

PRENEZ GARDE

Terence de Vere White

PRENEZ GARDE
'If Sinn Fein had its way there would be no more visits to
Mrs Heber, no more tennis for Miss Morris, no Bank for
Uncle Lindy, no job in Court for my father, no King, no
Queen, no Prince of Wales, no visits to Dublin to buy Christmas
presents and have tea at Mitchells in Grafton Street.
Everything would be given up to men in black hats and
trench coats with badges in their button-holes and cigarettes
behind their ears.'

Nine-year-old Brian was living in a time of fearful political
disturbance — though he was not supposed to be aware of
it. The solicitous parental warning ''prenez garde de l'enfant''
could not exclude the atmosphere of Ireland in the troubled
1920s. Seen through Brian's eyes, PRENEZ GARDE tells of
horrible happenings (did the Black and Tans really skin babies
alive?); soul-destroying remorse (Brian believes he might
have committed two murders . . . not to mention adultery!);
and romantic dreams (if only the lovely Miss Morris would
wait for Brian to be 21) . . .

'Beautifully cool and wistful. A rare and intensely personal
kind of re-creation'
GUARDIAN

'Very enjoyable. Deliciously funny'
SCOTSMAN

'A charming and witty novel'
PUNCH

Futura Publications
Fiction
ISBN 0 7088 2944 9

PRIVILEGED CHILDREN

Frances Vernon

Winner of the Author's Club Award for Best First Novel

When Diana Molloy dies in 1912 she leaves her fourteen-year-old daughter, Alice, a curious inheritance — her collection of books and a lasting attachment to her mother's bohemian friends. Much to the self-possessed young Alice's dismay, she is packed off to a rural vicar uncle — but it is not long before she contrives her escape to the Bloomsbury life she loved.

Flourishing in London once more, she is free to make her own life and to develop her talent as a painter. But as the troubles of the Great War approach, the free thinkers and artists who have become her 'family' find their own conflict as they struggle to maintain their principles of pacifism and communal economy. And then Alice is faced with the unexpected rebellion of her own daughter, Finola, who seeks a more conventional life.

'Here is genuine sparkle and invention'
DAILY EXPRESS

'Reminds one of Nancy Mitford, or of Daisy Ashford grown up'
THE PEN

Futura Publications
Fiction
ISBN 0 7088 2842 6

SUMMER AT THE HAVEN

Katharine Moore

Mrs Thornton lives in the attic because she prefers it.
Surrounded by intimate memorials of her past, she counts
her blessings:

. . . she is not deaf, like old Miss Brown
. . . nor going blind, like Miss Norton
. . . nor arthritic like Miss Dawson
. . . nor bald, like Miss Ford
. . . nor bronchial like Mrs Perry
. . . nor (thank God) wandering in her mind, like Mrs Langley

For Mrs Thornton is one of the eight residents of The Haven,
a private home for elderly ladies, which, like its occupants,
has seen better times.

Shrewd, warm-hearted, funny, unsentimental, SUMMER AT
THE HAVEN is that rarest of novels: a book about old age
that shines with optimism.

Futura Publications
Fiction
ISBN 0 7088 2516 8

THE SUMMERHOUSE

Val Mulkerns

'A remarkable book, full of insight and feeling . . .'
EVENING PRESS

It crouched forlornly in the kitchen — a crumbling fretwork summerhouse, a symbol of failure and decay, perfectly appropriate to the family that drifted round its disintegrating form, sniping bitchily at each other.

Eleanor, beautiful, frustrated, feeding on her contempt for her spineless husband Con; Margaret, mother of Martin, slowly sinking back into the clinging folds of her family from which she had all too briefly escaped; their mother, senile and overbearing; Hanny, spinster daughter, finding her only satisfaction in eroding her sisters' confidence and self-image; and Ruth, Martin's wife, a crisp if timid observer of the lethal family minuet . . .

Told in the voices of five separate but intertwined characters, THE SUMMERHOUSE evokes the lives of an Irish family whose tragedies and occasional joys will haunt every reader.

'evocative'
THE IRISH PRESS

Futura Publications
Fiction
ISBN 0 7088 2623 7

THE BRIDE

Bapsi Sidhwa

On the run from justice, Qasim, a tribesman from the hills, comes across a lost child. Unable to abandon her to an inevitable fate, he names her Zaitoon and takes her with him to Lahore, where she is brought up content in her mindless role as a purdah-bound woman. Until — as he must — Qasim arranges her marriage.

As bride to one of Qasim's 'lawless' primitive tribesmen she is condemned to a harsh existence in the barren hills of the Himalayas, a life of utter subjugation. For a girl from the city it is hard to accept — and, only when her very life is at stake will Zaitoon find a means of escape.

'Delicate and lively . . . elegantly controlled'
OBSERVER

'Exotic cliffhanger . . . a marvellous feel for imagery'
FINANCIAL TIMES

Futura Publications
Fiction
ISBN 0 7088 2511 7

THE FIERCEST HEART

Stuart Cloete

Overcoming savage natives who oppose their advance,
surviving through fire, flood and disease, withstanding
treachery in their midst, the Boer Trekkers of the 1830s made
history.

THE FIERCEST HEART vividly tells the story of one such
group of Trekkers. Led by Willem Prinsloo they gather their
every possession and leave the security of their Cape Colony
home in search of a new Canaan far from British rule.

The enchanting Cina, Prinsloo's orphaned grand-daughter
travels with them. A beautiful questing child when they leave,
a woman — who has seen more than most do in a lifetime
— when they find their new home, she embodies the fiery
independence of the pioneer spirit.

A well-deserved classic of South African fiction THE FIERCEST
HEART is a powerful, colourful and passionate tale of the
courage and determination of a displaced people in search
of a new land.

Futura Publications
Fiction
ISBN 0 7088 2626 1